W9-BSN-991

THE WORK
IS INNOCENT

Also by *Rafael Yglesias*

HIDE FOX, AND ALL AFTER

THE WORK
IS
INNOCENT

Rafael Yglesias

MIDDLEBURY COLLEGE LIBRARY

DOUBLEDAY & COMPANY, INC.
GARDEN CITY, NEW YORK
1976

PS
3575
G53
W6

7/1977
Am. Lit.

Library of Congress Cataloging in Publication Data

Yglesias, Rafael, 1954–
The work is innocent.

I. Title.
PZ4.Y53Wo [PS3575.G53] 813'.5'4
ISBN: 0-385-00965-8
Library of Congress Catalog Card Number: 74-2530

Copyright © 1976 by Rafael Yglesias
ALL RIGHTS RESERVED
PRINTED IN THE UNITED STATES OF AMERICA
FIRST EDITION

For My Parents

Throughout his later boyhood and into his earlier manhood the youth is always striving away from his home and the things of it. With whatever pain he suffers through the longing for them, he must deny them; he must cleave to the world and the things of it; that is his fate, that is the condition of all achievement and advancement for him. He will be many times contemptible, he will be mean and selfish upon occasion; but he can scarcely otherwise be a man; the great matter for him is to keep some place in his soul where he shall be ashamed. Let him not be afraid of being too unsparing in his memories; the instinct of self-preservation will safeguard him from showing himself quite as he was. No man, unless he puts on the mask of fiction, can show his real face or the will behind it. For this reason the only real biographies are the novels, and every novel, if it is honest, will be the autobiography of the author and the biography of the reader.

—William Dean Howells
Years of My Youth

THE WORK
IS INNOCENT

CHAPTER ONE

He called them the Dark Years. And pictured them thus: he would vomit out his intimate feelings to each person he met (imagining it was his soul he revealed), was quickly humiliated by having done so, and then spat where his vomit lay. All this, and the poor victim was never allowed a response.

But his judgment was too harsh. His compulsion to confess was not like vomiting, it was like masturbation. The humiliation was real, though it came from the mistake of believing his confession was disgusting; only the anger is accurately described. But this image encouraged him to continue the destructive cycle, since it was romantic. A wonderfully violent character creating altars of vomit and saliva, rather than the truth: a perverse boy producing pools of watery-white liquid.

The previous spring, when Richard Goodman was thrown out of a New York prep school, he begged his parents to allow him to live in Vermont with his sister, brother-in-law, and niece, and go to school there. He was afraid of being knifed in a New York public high school. Since his parents had decided to move to Vermont permanently, they figured Richard might as well start early in the high school where he would have to finish his last three years.

He had managed to reach the Christmas holidays without cutting, but in January his addiction to Balzac had resulted in five days of staying home. His parents had warned that failure would mean an immediate summons to New York, so Richard knew what awaited him when his brother-in-law, John, answered the phone and told Richard to come and speak with his father.

The entire affair seemed so ritualized and predictable that it assumed theatrical proportions causing Richard to imagine that his slow movements to the phone were observed by an audience impressed with the contempt he showed for his fate.

The kitchen had only one pale yellow light, and it added to the dreariness of the scene. His father was terse, telling him to get on the next flight to New York. Richard asked if he might stay for the weekend and was given permission. That ended the call, not unlike one to a travel agency. Yet after hanging up, an explosion of sweat betrayed his calm and Richard lost himself in that sickly light, harassed and nauseated by the countryside's loud buzzing silence.

After waiting for either Naomi, his sister, or John to call out asking what had happened, but getting no such question, Richard sought them out. They were on the living-room couch, John's arm around Naomi. She looked at Richard with concern, love, and confidence, but John's eyes asked: "Can you survive this?"

"Well, the man has called," Richard said. "I must go."

"Really?" John asked.

"I go Monday. Dad said you should pay for my ticket and he'll send you a check for it."

"They're going to have you go to school there?" Naomi asked.

"Didn't say a word about it."

"I'm surprised they did it," John said.

"Oh, come on. They had to." Richard smiled at both of them to communicate his awareness of every move his parents might make. He looked through the doorway to his bedroom and saw the typewriter with page ninety-eight of his novel in it.

He realized that his calm came from it. "That's gonna get me out of this," he said.

Naomi looked pleased. "What page are you on?"

"I think I'm almost halfway done."

"Did you tell them about it?" John asked.

"No. I told you I wasn't going to tell them about it until it's done. I mean it's gonna seem crazy enough to them when I present it finished."

"I don't think it's gonna seem crazy," Naomi said. "It's really good."

"No, no. I don't mean that. I mean letting me drop out of school because of my writing it will seem crazy." Richard watched them. They had read his novel almost page by page since he had begun it three months before and they had told him it was terrific. But he never tired of checking. "You know I think Mom and Dad are gonna like it," he said, playing the coquette.

John nodded. "Oh yeah. I think it'll really give them pause."

Richard was delighted. "That's what I wanna give them. Pause." He laughed. "You know, if I can pull them inside my life. That should be heavy for them. For the world."

John made a noise. "Uh. Little Richard's gettin' carried away with himself."

"Well, I have to feel that way, right? I mean I couldn't write if I thought about it like it's a cute hobby."

"No, that's cool," John said earnestly. "But the world's gonna give you a little fight on that. They're not just gonna concede it to you."

Naomi disengaged herself from John. "But that's not important, is it?" she asked. "I mean you're doing what you want to do. Most people can't, you know?" She looked at Richard plaintively. "It doesn't matter what the world says."

"Oh yes, it does!" He smiled briefly to impress her with the importance of being realistic. "Unless the world relates to it I won't be published or make money." This didn't seem to convince Naomi. "I mean how do you go on writing when you're broke?"

"Oh, that's such bullshit. I'm sorry but that's nonsense.

3

Plenty of writers have had a job while writing. Most of them have. Haven't they?"

Richard laughed. "First you say so, then you ask. Tolstoy didn't, Dickens didn't, Balzac, Dostoevsky, Eliot—"

"Richard, you can't bring up those people all the time. I mean today. There are very few writers who earn a living—"

"Yeah, they have a job. They teach a fuckin' English course for thirty-thousand a year."

"I don't mean those people. That's not who you want to be."

"I'd like to," John said.

"No, I don't want to be them," Richard said. "But that's unusual."

"Richard! Why are you being so silly?" Naomi was flushed. "You can't expect Mom and Dad to support you while you write."

"Who said I expected them to?"

"Then you'll have to get a job. And it won't be in a college." She was suddenly sorry for her vehemence. "Right? I mean. You know what I mean."

"Okay, so I have to get a lousy job. What's the point?"

"There's no point!"

Richard looked at John, exasperated. "Then what are you saying to me," he yelled.

"Whoa," John said. "Everybody be cool."

"Oh, God!" Naomi jumped up from the couch. "What's the matter with everybody?" She was naturally thin and nervous, and anger seemed too strong a feeling for her body to support. "I just mean that you shouldn't believe that bullshit that you have to be pampered in order to write. You can write holding a lousy job."

The baby wailed from the other room. Naomi glanced in its direction fiercely. "I'll handle it," John said. He moved past her, but she stopped him by taking his arm. "No," she said, and Richard was amazed by the tones she put in the word: anger, frustration, apology, and love. Richard's niece upset him with desperate, choking cries. Naomi stood still, her eyes blank and staring. She scratched an eyebrow thoughtfully until she seemed calmer and then went inside.

John picked up the graph paper on the table in front of him and went into the kitchen. Richard followed him. John said, "What was that about?"

Richard said, "I don't know," but he felt that dulled depression which followed certain kinds of arguments with his family. Naomi loathed the cynicism of literary people and believed real artists were strong, honest persons who had to forsake the ease and decadence of middle-class New York life, who should purge themselves by living among poor and working-class Americans.

She had left home at eighteen when Richard was only seven years old, and he remembered the fearful bulletins his mother had received: she was hitchhiking across the country, working as a waitress in greasy spoons; she was in Mississippi with the civil rights movement when the three whites were murdered and redneck night patrols taking potshots were common.

He envied her courage; he was stunned she could give up a comfortable bed, much less risk her life. And he had no contempt for her still maintaining those principles now that she was married and had a child, living in a house on one hundred acres of beautiful land.

But he had kept guiltily guarded his amendment to her views: he believed goodness in people was achieved by such sacrifice, but he knew that literary genius required only egotism and talent. In life great writers were fools or scoundrels.

John followed the evening routine. He cleared the table for his designs, sharpened the pencils, and poured himself a glass of wine. He had managed to develop an excellent reputation as a designer and builder, though he had had no formal architectural training. Richard wondered at the meticulous drawings, never able to picture the structures they represented. He watched John's reflection in the old lead-glass windows: John's full black beard and his plump English face were ghostly against the shimmery background.

When Richard poured himself a glass of wine, John looked up with a smile. "I thought you weren't going to drink any more."

"Well, I'm leaving. You know, celebration. Why? You don't want me to?"

"Oh no. I'm glad. I like to have company." He leaned back and scratched the sides of his beard. "How's the book going?"

"Fine. I'm almost at the end of that day."

"Oh, I meant to tell you. That was good having them feel sleepy. It reminds you that it's all been one day." He sipped his wine and looked at Richard appraisingly. "How come you thought of doing it that way?"

"Because of *The Idiot*. Dostoevsky's novel. The first two hundred pages of it are one day. In a conventional narrative. 'Cause avant-garde people do like ten minutes for a thousand pages. Anyway, his thing was fantastic so I thought I'd make the first half just action when life is exhilarating for the main character."

John grunted and nodded. Richard knew that reserve was typical of John, but he always feared that he had made a fool of himself when it occurred.

Richard tried to drink the sour wine without losing his sense and talking wildly. John remained calm no matter how much he drank, at worst becoming sluggish, but never hysterical or incoherent. He worked patiently, even smoking his cigarettes with deliberate smooth motions.

"What do you think are its chances of being published?" John asked without warning, hunched over his work. Richard knew that he would look up in a moment, his eyes evaluating without malice.

"Well, since it will have nothing to do with quality the only question is whether or not it will seem commercial to them." John nodded and Richard smiled at him. "So? It's written by a fifteen-year-old about a kid who drops out and smokes dope, right? Only thing I'm missing is sex." John opened his mouth in a silent laugh, a cloud of cigarette smoke escaping with it. "In life and in the novel. But I really don't know what its chances are. It's supposed to be impossible to publish a first novel."

"You're not really worrying about it?"

"How can I?"

6

"No. You shouldn't. It would probably just be confusing to think about. You know?" John looked into his eyes. "I really think it's good."

"Yeah?"

John sipped his wine and returned it to the table. "Yeah." Richard knew this was high praise and he was pleased.

Naomi came in with Nana in her arms. Richard's niece looked at him with puffed, drugged eyes and gladly gave herself up to John's embrace. Naomi held herself stiffly and stared at Richard. "Do you know what I meant?" she asked, as if there had been no interval.

The men laughed. "When is it, uh, going to get to the boot-throwing exhibition?" John asked.

"Come on, John," Naomi said, sounding dangerous.

"It wasn't a boot," Richard said. "It was an ashtray that she threw at me."

"I was down in the cellar and it sounded as if it was more than one thing."

"Yeah, I threw *Cousine Bette* at her. A literary argument."

"You don't understand the relationship Richard and I have, John." Naomi had relaxed but she was still serious. "We were always the fighters in the family. Right?"

"Yeah," Richard agreed. "You think that's good?"

"Oh yeah! Sure. It's just because we're being honest with each other."

"Okay. So then what was your question?"

John got up, stroking Nana's arm. He said, "I'd better get out of the way of the honesty." He walked out slowly while Richard giggled.

"I don't want to fight," Naomi said.

"Neither do I."

She looked at him earnestly. "I just meant—you know—I wanted you not to get into thinking you can't survive unless you go to school."

"I want to drop out. How can you say that to me?"

"Wait! *Or*—I don't know. I mean you can work, you know? You don't have to be pampered."

"I agree with you."

"Are you sure? What if Mom and Dad—well, what if your novel doesn't get published? You know you can't expect it to. You plan to get some shitty, shitty job like you'll have to get?"

"Yeah. I'll have to."

"You think you could do that?"

"Why couldn't I?"

"I think you can. But you've never done it before."

"I've never written a novel before."

"Come on! There's a difference."

"Yeah, there's a difference in how much I enjoy it. But writing isn't easier than doing work. I think one can assume if I'm capable of writing, then I'm capable of working."

"That's a myth!" Naomi was on her feet suddenly, enraged. "It's bullshit that writing is more difficult than work."

"I didn't say that! I didn't say it was more difficult. I was saying they were equal."

She looked at him, puzzled for a moment. "Okay," she said, her anger gone. "But that's the myth everyone believes. That some bullshit intellectual is doing something more important or difficult than a carpenter. Aaron"—her voice rose, Richard knowing what was to follow on hearing his father's name— "will talk about an intellectual he doesn't even admire as if he's doing something more important than working people. Unless they have what he calls ideas, they're not a human being. That's so sickening."

"I agree with you." His tone begged her to stop. He had heard this before and took it seriously. Richard had also suffered indignation at his father's statements: though Aaron attacked intellectuals for ignoring oppressed people, he held them up as models for Richard's career. It had been good to hear Naomi reject it. But with repetition he felt it was wrong. "I agree with you," he repeated quietly, reining her in. "But you confuse everything with the generalizations you make. You're not talking about intellectuals, you're talking about academicians. Real intellectuals you admire. Beckett is an intellectual."

"Oh, that's wrong!"

"That's not wrong. Intellectual means someone who concerns himself with ideas, and Beckett does that. Dad isn't an intellectual. What has he ever said that could be classified as a philosophy? What has he ever said—in ideas—about man's condition on earth? Zero. Dad's a playwright. Playwrights aren't intellectuals. They can be, but not necessarily so. Just because society has called anyone not doing shit work an intellectual doesn't mean you should confuse those terms also."

"I don't know what you're talking about, Richard."

"Why not?"

"That's bullshit. I don't care if you call them different things. I don't care who is or isn't an intellectual. Beckett may be concerned with ideas, but that's not what I like him for."

"What do you like about him then?"

"Because—" Naomi paused while her anger settled. "I can't describe it."

"Try and tell me anyway."

"It's not an idea, some kind of philosophy. It's what he says about Time—"

"That's an—"

"I don't mean as an idea. He does it the way it feels and that's not some crappy intellectualism. Or the way they speak in *Godot*, that's exactly the way people talk when they're really, really stoned. And that doesn't have to do with any shit about man—"

"Naomi! More than any other playwright, Beckett's form is suited—is created with the sole idea of allowing philosophical ideas to exist as characters. He's the most obviously intellectual playwright I've ever read. You know that. Just because you use the word and it's implanted in your mind as meaning nonsense, you won't admit that someone you like is an intellectual."

"You're just throwing words at me. I'm not arguing semantics!"

"Oh, for crying out loud. Because I'm talking about words you think it's meaningless."

She looked contemptuously angry. "This is silly."

"That's a lot like Dad, you know. To dismiss an argument when losing it."

9

Naomi grabbed the chair in front of her and lifted it up. Her head jerked away from him and then back. She slammed the chair down. "This isn't a game!" she yelled, tears coming without delay. "I'm not playing. People don't win and lose, Richard."

She had the capacity, as did all the members of his family, to make him feel he was crude and unsympathetic. He fought the feeling on instinct, but he feared it was true that he preferred to be right rather than to be kind. "Don't pull that shit on me. I'm not scared by that fucking chair shit."

"I'M NOT TRYING TO SCARE YOU," she screamed, and frightened him into silence.

"Hey, hey." John came running in. "Nana's asleep. Just be cool in here, huh?"

Naomi stamped her bare foot on the floor, her eyes red with rageful tears. "Damn it," she said, and walked inside to her room.

Richard felt the pressure and embarrassment of the sudden silence. He trembled trying to light a cigarette: his fury was liquid in his body and it pumped with dangerous force. He was angry about so many things. His lack of control, the refusal of anyone in his family to listen to his opinions, Naomi's stupidity, his father's egotism. There was no way to organize the emotional contradictions behind them. How could he be angry over a failure in his family to have a consistent line on intellectuals? It was absurd to care.

But they browbeat him with their stupid distinctions.

He had heard everything they believed. His father's love of manners and the proper use of English while he attacked capitalism and doctrinaire Communism; his insistence that American writing was vital and interesting, though he attacked most American writers. His brother, Leo, called American intellectuals pigs and ghouls, though he devoted much of his time to reading them; Leo had an extraordinary background of reading in black history, and he used it to abort any opinions Richard might venture on politics. Richard was shut up because he misused a word, or because he based his judgments on racist history books. Whenever he read a book they recommended and he wished to discuss a judgment of theirs, back came this response: "Oh, wait until you read so and so. Then you'll see what I mean."

He loved them and had listened to every idea, great and foolish, they told him. He wanted to be respected in turn. He expected to achieve that with his novel. So he used it as an outlet for the tremendous rage that his argument with Naomi had left with him. He worked until early morning and had forgotten the roots of his inspiration when he fell asleep.

On Monday morning it was snowing. While driving to the airport he hoped the flight would be canceled. Brother and sister, who had casually apologized to each other for their quarrel, were tired and not talkative. John was cheerful. He handled the four-wheel-drive truck easily, Richard fascinated by his competence. The sight was familiar: John's ski boot pumping the brakes, his hand appearing at the end of his overlarge white knit sweater, reaching into his shirt pocket for a pack of cigarettes, emerging and tipping the pack so that he could catch one with his lips. There was never any desperation or awkwardness in the movement; sharp curves never disturbed it.

Richard openly admired John's physical confidence. He had studied him carefully and guessed that they were learned, not intuitive, gestures. Richard had told him his suspicion and John had laughed, delighted. He admitted that as an adolescent he had worked on such things and it had become habitual. "But now you pay no attention to it?" Richard had asked.

But John wasn't sure. "Well, I don't have to work at the movements, like when I was a teen-ager. But I'm always aware of what I'm doing."

"Everybody is aware of their movements, right?"

"I don't think so. Lots of people don't go through that stuff. They just breeze through life. They do their number and there's no problem with it."

It sounded so pleasant just to breeze through life. It was a squalling storm for Richard, every gesture a mortal decision. "You know, John, I don't think that's true. I think it's like everything else. Everybody thinks they're the only person who masturbates or talks to themselves, et cetera. Right?"

"I don't think so," he insisted. "It's special."

John's physical grace was certainly rare, and Richard appreciated its refinements as if it were a grand ballet. So he was well entertained during the drive.

John and Naomi were staying at the house his parents had bought and planned to move into. During the winter John was supposed to make a bedroom out of the unfinished attic, and their only conversation was caused by Richard's question about it. "Should I tell Mom and Dad what you've done so far, or would you rather it be a surprise?"

"Either way."

"Richard," Naomi said with alarming seriousness, "what are you going to do if they make you go to school?"

"I'm going to run away."

John said mildly, "You will do that, huh?"

"Yep."

Naomi looked incredulously at them. "What's going on? How come this is so casual? 'I'm going to run away. Oh, really?' " Her imitation was good humored.

"We've talked about it," John said.

"And you weren't going to mention it to me?" Naomi asked Richard.

"I was afraid you were going to tell me to get a job."

They laughed. Naomi said, "You can't run away to us, you know."

Richard was hurt. "Don't say that."

"I'm sorry," Naomi said quickly. She patted him on the shoulder. "I mean I'd be happy to have you stay with us. I just mean we can't because of Aaron and Betty."

"Don't you think I'd realize that? What kind of fool do you think I am?"

"Okay, listen. I'm sorry. I didn't mean that." She began to cry, and Richard was suddenly full of feeling for her. "Let's make up," she said. He mumbled, sure, and kissed her on a red cheek.

"Your nose is so cold," he said, and they laughed to be rid of their embarrassment.

"Really a sick relationship," John said.

"You just don't understand," Naomi said.

"I'm kidding."

"So, Richard," Naomi asked tentatively, "where would you go?"

"Well, remember when Mac called me? He's at college in Boston and he invited me to stay with him."

"For free?"

"No," Richard said, his tone sarcastic. "I have to get a job."

"Oh boy," John said, laughing.

"Okay." Naomi was still afraid of the conversation. "I don't mean about getting a job or anything. I just mean about breaking with Mom and Dad. Are you really able to do that?"

He wished she hadn't forced him to think about it. "I don't know. Probably not. But I'm not ready to submit either." He looked at her significantly. "Get it?"

CHAPTER TWO

Richard got off his plane, prepared to greet his parents, and was unpleasantly surprised to see his brother, Leo, waving to him from the top of the escalator that came out onto the main lobby of La Guardia Airport. His brother looked down at him casually and, once noticed, turned aside to drag on the butt of his cigarette in the Bogart manner. Richard's surprise was overcome in watching his brother's movements, and when he reached the end of the escalator, it had changed to amazed scorn for the naïveté of his parents. Could they really still be unaware of his contempt for Leo?

The baggage was late in coming and concern over it—his novel!—delayed conversation. Richard nearly gave away its existence because of anxiety, and if he was that careless, he wondered if he could conceal his desire to run away. Once in the cab, Leo asked, "So how was the flight?"

"Shabby. Very shabby. The jets go up like helicopters. Straight up. I really thought I was going to vomit."

"Do you usually get sick on planes?"

"No. For some reason this was incredibly bad. It's one of those small jets and it kicked around like a motherfucker."

Leo grunted and looked out his window. Richard followed

suit but for him it had real interest. From the grace and bounty of the countryside to the decay of New York. They were nearing home, and seeing the bloodthirsty streets of his neighborhood so frightened him that it seemed impossible he had ever walked them without terror.

"How do you feel about coming back?" Leo asked.

"How do you think I feel?"

"I don't know. Why don't you tell me?"

Richard laughed. "I feel it is disastrous. I cannot imagine anything more loathsome."

"You really feel that way?"

"Uh, yeah. You havin' trouble believing me?"

"No. You said it—I thought you were kidding." Leo had cut his hair short, and his friendly, startled eyes were even more so. "You know Brandeis isn't so bad."

"What's Brandeis?"

"The high school you're going to go to."

"I didn't know I was going to one."

"Are you kidding, man?" Richard had convinced himself of his power, so this coup was a shock. He wasn't able to conceal his disappointment, and Leo looked at him sadly. "It's good there. There are dyno blacks, and you can do some really good organizing."

Richard retreated into contempt. "If I wanted to get into organizing, I'd prefer to do it outside of school."

"Yeah, sure, but it's better to be going to that kind of a school than to some kind of white bullshit like Cabot. Or to something so unreal like the school in Vermont."

Richard wanted to jeer at Leo for his pitiful adulation of blacks, for the absurd conclusions it led him into—but they had arrived. His mother had made a good lunch, and the talk was lively. His situation wasn't mentioned, but he enjoyed himself so much that his resolve to run away was weakened.

His mother showed him to his room, proud of how neat she had made it. Richard, though pleased, was uneasy that his things had been gone through.

"It's lovely," he told her. "But you didn't have to. I would have enjoyed doing it."

"Oh, it was a lot of fun. Richard, I can't tell you how it broke my mother's heart, going through your drawers."

Richard flashed silence with his eyes so expressively that Betty almost jumped. Her smile disappeared and her tone changed. "You know. All the broken ashtrays."

He quieted and said that he had no other way of disposing of them, since he shouldn't have been smoking.

"You could have sneaked them into the garbage."

"Yeah I guess so. Listen, I want to change."

She turned to leave but asked instead, "How are Naomi and John?"

"Like I said. Fine."

Betty narrowed her eyes at him. Richard smiled. He felt uncomfortable. "Is there some reason, something you think is wrong between them?" he asked.

"No," she said. "I was just looking at my son." Richard laughed and she smiled. "How's my little girl Nana?"

"As cute as ever."

"Is she walking all over the place?"

"All over the place."

"Good. Oh, I want to see her!"

"You will pretty soon."

"Do you need any help unpacking?"

"No, that's all right."

"Did Leo tell you about Brandeis?"

"That I'll be going there? Yes, he did."

"We have to go on Thursday to sign you up."

"When does school start?"

"A week from today. So you have a little vacation."

"Great," he said, drawling the word sarcastically. He watched her exit, and when the door closed behind her, the flush of embarrassment he had repressed overwhelmed him. He went over to the drawers and looked through them. His collection of *Playboys* and photogenic women had been uncovered and carefully rearranged. It had been his garbage heap: typing paper covering broken ashtrays, covering pornography, covering grass. He had left none of the last in the drawer, his only consolation. He felt he had risen above the meanness of this past suddenly and laughed at its revelation, only to relapse again into a little boy's shame. Work, he said to himself, work and you'll forget it.

During the next few days, his parents must have wondered at the serenity of his schedule. He rose early, had breakfast, retired to his room, and began typing. Aaron joked that he must be working on a novel. When Richard admitted it matter-of-factly, Aaron opened his eyes wide and looked serious. "Writing is less profitable than acting, if such a thing is possible. Have you given that up?"

"I didn't know that I had it to give up," Richard said.

Aaron looked playfully at his wife. "I think our son's becoming a wit. Are we going to get a chance to read it?"

"I was going to ask Mom."

"Quite right," Aaron said, bowing his head, which showed his longish, graying hair to advantage. "The editor first."

Richard didn't think of his mother the way the world did: the magazine for which she was the literary editor was small and printed on rough, ugly paper; its grandiose name, *The Union*, struck him as laughable. Betty had worked there for some years before Richard found out from others that its prestige was great. But he respected her opinion for intimate reasons. He thought of both his parents as extraordinary minds whose literary judgments were particularly formidable.

He knew she was a quick reader, and when he heard her making warning coughs as she approached his room only a half hour after he gave her the manuscript, he expected the worst. He rushed to his desk, lit a cigarette, and in an attempt to seem carefree, tilted his chair back so violently that he had to leap up to avoid splitting his head open. Betty found him like that. "Did I startle you?"

"No. I just nearly killed myself on that chair." Richard became very absorbed in moving the chair about and pressing down on it as if the floor might give way.

"You were leaning back?"

"Yes, yes. I know. You've always warned me. But, uh, my

work." Richard despaired of the chair being any more of a distraction, so he resigned himself to sitting in it. He looked at his mother standing solemnly in front of him, holding the manuscript. She shifted her weight from one foot to the other and said, "Well, Richard—"

"Oh, God," he mumbled.

She tilted her head up questioningly. She looked old.

"Nothing," he said. "Go on." He lunged for his cigarette in the ashtray and burst out with, "What did you think?"

"It's great," she said so simply that he was tempted to take it as an insult. "It's lovely. I'm very impressed."

"Is that it?"

She relaxed and laughed. "Isn't that enough?"

He followed her movements to the bed where she sat down. "No, I didn't mean that. I mean wasn't anything wrong with it?"

"Not really. It needs some polishing."

"Well, it's a first draft."

"Of course. That's the kind of work it needs. Silly things. You've misspelled some words in such a funny way."

"Okay. I don't want to hear that."

"It's fine. This is only half the novel. So I don't know what you're going to do with it." She tapped her foot thoughtfully and looked around the room dully. "It's very strong and surprising. Reminds one of the real way it felt to be young. That's very unusual."

Her tone was full of the shock of recognition, and it acted like a strong purgative on the awkward and insecure feelings he had for his work.

"So," she said, turning her eyes on him and narrowing them. "You mean to publish this?"

"You make it sound like it's up to me. I hope to."

"If the rest is as good, then I think you have a real chance. But," she said, laughing while she repeated a family joke, "don't get your hopes up."

He smiled but held her eyes and put force in his tone. "Good enough to get me out of school?"

Betty looked at the large poster of Che on the wall opposite the bed. A cigar was comfortably tucked into the corner of his mouth and his eyes glittered with mischief. She was not surprised by his question. There was a silence. Richard felt a mad compulsion to wink at Che.

"You want to finish this, get it published, and then what?" Richard frowned, leaped for his cigarette, dragged on it, and hastily pressed it out. "Write more."

"Come on, Richard. You're fifteen. It's just crazy to settle down at that age to a life of writing."

"I'm sick of going over this. I'm willing to do other things, but not go to high school. I'm willing to get a job, anything but that."

"Okay. Okay. What about college?"

"College means high school first. So forget it."

"I mean that if we sent this manuscript to some people at Columbia to see if they can get you in."

"Are you kidding? That would be great."

"We can try," she said, getting up and approaching the desk slowly. "I can't imagine what else they might want."

"Then do you think it's really good?"

She smiled and lowered his manuscript to the desk. "You're as bad as your father. You don't even want to go to school until you're sixteen?"

"Mom, truancy is a joke in New York. Leo can tell you that."

"Some recommendation."

"Well, you can forget about trying to get me to go to high school. I just won't do it."

"Richie, you don't have to threaten me. I want your father to read this and then we'll talk about it."

The wait for his father to finish reading was ghastly. Not because the school issue depended on his opinion; Aaron had disapproved of most of his actions lately and Richard had been used to getting his greatest encouragement from him. The lack of it had upset him more than he knew.

Richard and Betty waited in the kitchen and Richard continued to describe John's work nervously while he heard his father approaching. He stopped in mid-sentence and looked at Aaron when he entered and sat down. When he had written papers for school, or been in its theater productions, his father would congratulate him noisily, with hugs and unbounded predictions for his future. It was pleasing but never allowed Richard to think that he had achieved a permanent, adult success. He had tried to force that recognition and failed, losing also paternal delight.

"Well," Aaron said as if the word had meaning. He looked at Richard, his eyes glittering with feeling. Richard was embarrassed by its intimacy. "You rotten kid." He looked at Betty and she smiled.

"It's good, isn't it?" she asked.

"What's extraordinary is the narrative line. It's so sophisticated. You'd think this was his eighth novel. Are you sure you know what you're doing?" he asked playfully.

"Yeah, I know." Richard was insistent.

Aaron laughed and grabbed his shoulder, shaking him with his pleasure. "I'm kidding. It's great. I think you might have some trouble with the scene you're working on."

"Oh no. I have that planned. I know what I'm doing."

Aaron laughed again and got up. "Come on. Let me give you a hug." Richard did so reluctantly but almost burst into tears in his embrace. "Well, if you've written this you certainly don't need any encouragement."

His parents had a long private conference and then announced to him that he would not have to finish high school. They wanted him to finish the book and send it to both publishers and universities.

For a month he worked and was close to being done. It was peaceful, at first, to do nothing else. But soon the studied elegance of the apartment, of his life, added to the monkishness of his celibacy.

He was sixteen, and no amount of talent or imagination could make a woman's vagina real for him. He didn't know what it looked like. He laughed at the idea but the truth was inescapable—*he had not seen or felt one.* And that neat business with the penis, though he had a dim sense of it, still seemed a most unlikely and ridiculous thing to do. Homosexuality was as real as the metal of his typewriter: just as grubby and unyielding. Oh sure, he had never fucked that way, but it was imaginable. And it was that truth that made him unable to shrug off this renewed fear of being homosexual as being typically adolescent.

How could he pretend to the manliness of being published without fucking (one way or the other)? Without being cool and breezy with women: the pleasant nudging of his father's charm or the uncomplicated exuberance with which his brother posed his body for women.

He decided this isolation and passivity, however grand in intention, were perverse. So he called an old friend from Cabot. He traveled through time more than space, but there it was: to lose one's virginity, one had to be an adolescent.

"May I speak to Raul, please?"

After a long silence an unrecognizable voice answered.

"Raul? This is Richard."

"Richard? Uh. Who?"

"Richard Goodman. From Cabot."

"Oh! How come you're calling?"

"I've been in Vermont for about a year and I just wanted to be in touch again."

"In touch again. I see you still have that stiffness."

"Well, I feel uncomfortable. I've cut myself off from all my friends. But no one can live that way, so you can't blame me for trying."

"Yeah. Well, I left, you know, so I haven't been seeing the old crowd either."

"No loss, I guess. So they finally threw you out?"

"Not exactly, but more or less. Fuck it. Let's not talk about Cabot. I'm in Performing Arts now. Are you going to school in Vermont?"

"I'm not going to school at all."

"Huh? Are you living with your parents?"

"Oh, I'm not crashing and on the run and dealing dope in the Village. I'm the affluent dropout."

"Shit, I thought I was the only one from Cabot who'd have that privilege."

"Naw. I was just quieter about it than you were."

"Hey! We're on the phone for a minute and you're insulting me?"

Richard's boyish face absorbed this with difficulty. "I'm sorry. I really didn't mean that."

"Don't get maudlin. Listen. It's a guess, but are you all alone in this wonderful city and you'd like to enter the wonderful world of society?"

"It sounds pitiful but that's it." There was a silence. "I wish I could make it less puppyish."

"Aw, Richard, you are a puppy. You're cute. You should play that up with chicks. They like that. Okay, it's crazy, but there's a party tomorrow night. Can you smoke dope?"

"Yes," Richard said without humor.

"Terrific. So I'll give you—no, we'll go together and I'll do the honors." So at this price of humiliation Richard began his hunt.

He left the orderliness of his room, he left the life of the mind and went out onto the busy, decadent streets of New York. He held his arms against his plump body and swung his torso from side to side in a rocking motion. He was terrified that one of the many mad people who were talking to themselves and waving their arms distractedly would address him; that he would be suspected of a thousand crimes and seized by one of those obese monstrosities with their wooden-handled heavy guns. He walked carelessly to defy these terrors but would betray himself by jumping at loud noises and by his many stops to check street numbers. Even they could conspire against him.

He was to meet Raul at a coffee shop near the party about an hour before they were due to arrive. It seemed impossible that he found it easily and that Raul was waiting for him calmly. Raul's hair was very long and he looked skinnier and paler than seemed healthy.

"Do you believe it?" Raul said as a greeting. "I'm pleased by

the sight of you. I'm beginning to think fondly of that god-
damn school."

"I remind you of it. I can't say that you do. You look very
different."

"More degenerate. I know. I've started to get worried along
with my mother."

They ordered dinner and reminisced. The last was difficult:
neither knew of the fates of any of their friends, and since they
hadn't been close, there were few memories. Richard finally
screwed up his courage and asked what kind of people would
be at the party.

"Performing Arts kids mostly. You know, they're all artists.
How are you about that? Or are you most interested in law?"

Richard considered giving up his novel to the mercy of this
hysterical, flip creature, and decided against it. "What can I
say? With my father?"

"Oh yeah. That must make you a little disgusted with it all."

"I haven't been hit over the head with that Upper West
Side crowd too much. When they have their parties I stay in
the back room."

"I'd be right out there in the thick of it. How can you resist
it? With all those innuendoes it'd be great training. I mean,
unless you're going to be the first dropout professional you'll
have to make your way there."

"You're unwholesome, Raul," Richard said with more heat
than seemed normal. "If you really came in contact with it you
wouldn't like it."

Raul looked like a fox. "Sensitive subject with you, eh?
Okay, maybe I am unwholesome, whatever that means. But
that quiet, heartfelt tone of yours can't be real." Raul dragged
on his cigarette and leaned back as if relaxing. "Let's slow
down a little bit. All I really want to know is how are you going
to make money?"

"Is that so important?"

"Unhuh. Very important and you know it. How are you
going to eat dinner in ten years?"

Richard trembled and looked at the cars racing down the av-
enue. It was the taxis that he watched. From childhood they re-

23

tained a fascination for him: a New York child's idea of nobility. Our carriage to the ball. "I don't know," he said, reaffirming his decision not to talk about his novel. "Right now I'm just floating. I don't want to think about it."

Raul looked at him mildly, almost with sympathy. "I'm amazed your parents let you."

"They're okay about that stuff. They figure I can always get back on my feet."

"So you're on the lookout for a girl, right?" Raul sprang this on him as if he were a crack detective. The desired effect came about: Richard flushed and laughed nervously. "Okay," Raul said. "Some of these girls are in their twenties and even the Performing Arts girls will go all the way. *I* know that."

Richard could say nothing and Raul suggested they go. Raul's comment had scared him even more, and each step closer to the party added to his agony. Raul walked confidently and, when they reached the door, rang the bell so quickly and unexpectedly that Richard nearly cried out. He assumed a mother would come out, but a painted blonde flew into Raul's arms and then Raul's voice tumbled out an aria to the chorus of welcome from inside. Quickly they were in: it was all smoke and painted women and lanky men, everyone more knowing and powerful than he. "Can you relate to booze?" Raul was saying to his face. "Yes, liquor, I'm not kidding. We're not that new-fashioned."

A solemn girl with a long nose who took their coats said, "Turning phrases already?" She turned to Richard and addressed him more kindly than she had Raul. "We have things to drink if you're into that." Richard looked at her blankly so she smiled and said, "I'm Joan."

"He's Richard Goodman, son of playwright Aaron," Raul said. "He'll get eaten alive by all the actors here."

"Really?" the blonde said, excited. "Let me introduce myself."

A strikingly handsome young man yelled loudly, "Let's create a receiving line." Raul laughed and slapped his hand. He got them to lower the music. Announcing who Richard was, Raul took him by the arm and went around the room introducing all persons and their professional hopes. With the ensuing silence and calm, Richard was able to observe coolly. The men became more boyish and dumb, the women less affected, and he was free of his shock. The blonde, Ann, turned out to be quite plain and a little terrified of him, or rather of his father's reputation, and the handsome boy, to Richard's surprise, made no objection to Richard's being fat and Jewish. Indeed, he made an impression with his quiet seriousness and the stiff drink he downed effortlessly. Raul was drinking heavily and he held on too long to the joints that were being passed. He entertained the group with stories of Cabot, and his domination of the talk allowed Richard to become woozy from his second drink and the grass. When Raul went from being brilliant to incoherence and the party returned to listening to music, Richard had no difficulty responding to Joan when she asked if Raul and he were good friends.

"No. As a matter of fact, we never got along in Cabot. Raul was a winner even in failure, and I think he just had contempt for me."

A sandy-haired young man who had been introduced as a playwright sat down next to Richard. He had thin shoulder-length hair and with his metal-rimmed glasses looked like a poster of youth culture. "Did you feel the same way about him?"

Richard was surprised. "Contempt? No, I liked him. We just didn't get along."

"So, you haven't seen him in a while?" Joan asked.

"About eight or nine months."

"Is he different?"

Sandy-hair passed Richard a joint, and after taking a drag Richard felt encircled by silence, protected from the harsh music. "Do you love him?" he asked as if he were offering potato chips.

Neither of them was surprised by the question. "I don't know," Joan said. "We were a couple for a while."

"I hope you don't mind the question."

"You worry too much," she said quickly. She got up to leave. Richard barely heard her say those words. He knew what she had said but the sounds bounced off the glass bubble that was forming around him. He looked at Raul: he was waving his arms about and obviously talking loudly. His hysteria was ugly and irritating to Richard. Not caring if they heard, he said, "You're a lot like him. Very quick to judge. You're both so fuckin' clever." He got up and roughly pushed Joan aside, stepping over the people seated on the floor. The music was sex and corruption. He only wanted to be away from it. He went down a hallway, quiet and carpeted, disturbed a couple, and, confused by that, he walked quickly into a bedroom and shut the door.

Its silence was an institutions', but at least he was alone.

The grass had thrown him into a panic—he knew it, and the knowledge was redoubling his fear. He could feel himself going into the bad LSD trip of a few months ago. He was enclosed in the same antiseptic bubble. Of course, he knew it all came from his self-consciousness and alienation, but that hadn't stopped the onrush of panic that the trip would never end, that his true self was out.

"I'm a paranoid homosexual," he said, hoping to make a joke of it. But the walls, the carpet, the night were not amused. "It's very serious, isn't it?" He held his hands out and they looked long, powerful, and very real. "I don't care," he said to live up to the humanity of his hands. And at that moment it seemed as if he could beat it.

Joan came in meekly, frightening Richard. Had she heard? "I came to say I'm sorry," she said. "I really am. I'm sensitive about Raul. He hurt me."

Richard didn't know what to make of her about-face in attitude. He was relieved to have company and he said that the grass had made him jumpy. He regretted having snapped at her.

She sat down on the floor. "How adult we're being."

Richard smiled, feeling this was a compliment to his gravity of demeanor—something he prided himself on. "Raul," he said, "is an incredibly competitive person. You probably don't see it that way, but it comes out in his dealings with men. Particularly at Cabot."

"I don't think he's that crass."

"Crass?"

"You know, I gotta win. Low-level American mentality."

"Oh, he's clever and neurotic. At Cabot, once he started winning he lost interest in the game."

Joan nodded but said nothing.

Richard leaned back and smiled. "I'm putting him down and that's bothering you."

"Not exactly. There are good reasons why I should be putting him down. But I wouldn't like myself if I did. So I'd rather just not talk about him since he's an unpleasant subject."

"I'm sorry," Richard said. "Talking about him seems to be a good way of getting to know you."

"It's the worst way. He was a weird episode. Why don't you tell me about yourself?"

"I think I'll need a cigarette for that," he said, worried. He reached into his jacket pocket.

Joan said, "You're sweating. Why don't you take your jacket off?"

This second intimacy from her was disturbing. It was too naked a movement to remove the jacket and be left with only his blue Brooks Brothers shirt. He did it quickly without grace. "There's, uh, not much to say about my life. I left Cabot at the end of the ninth grade, spent the summer in Vermont, and went to school there until just about a month ago, and came here to New York."

"You didn't have a life before that?"

"Oh that," Richard said without irony. "I played a lot of slug. That's a kind of handball—"

"I know."

"Let's see. What else? I burned my room down when I was eight. That's pretty spectacular, isn't it?"

"It's heavy. Why did you burn it down?"

"Why?" The question floored him. He thought no detail of his life had been left unexplored but this seemed to be. The event was so dramatic that it needed no reason to exist. "You know, I was a child playing with matches. I had been burning paper behind radiators for a while. My parents caught me at it and warned me that I shouldn't do it again. We were also studying it at school."

Joan laughed. "It was a learning experience?"

Richard smiled with her. "It sure was. I had no idea of its potency." He laughed and pretended embarrassment. "Pardon me."

"Maybe that's what it was about," she suggested.

Now he was embarrassed. "I don't think so. Anyway I got some kitchen matches, went into my room, lit one, and not quite sure but at least telling myself that it was out, I dropped it into a wicker wastepaper basket. And left the room, shutting the door behind me. When I came back the room was completely in flames. I mean it was incredible. I don't see how it could have spread so quickly. I don't know why people always talk about the natural elements as being awesomely real. They're awesomely unreal. That's why we make up gods to explain them. Or chemical symbols. They're never explained in human terms." She looked at him, puzzled, and he felt a great urge to make her understand. "You relate to what I'm saying?"

"Well. I don't know. The natural elements exist outside of, uh, *us*. They shouldn't be explained in our terms."

"Listen. Since we're human, it's childish of us to explain things unless we explain them in terms of our perceptions. A flood is a great deal of water that drowns us, sweeps our homes away, tears up the land we've grown used to. Snow is white and it's very cold. It's soft for a while and then it hardens and becomes very dirty, like we do when we grow older."

"Life's better than that."

"I was exaggerating for effect."

"The way you talk about it, nothing changes. The way somebody first felt about rain is the only reasonable way for anyone to ever think about rain. That's too much to expect of people to never invent anything else. It's too boring."

Richard saw that it was futile explaining to her, that it was silly even to have made an attempt. "I guess so," he said with what he hoped was an ironic smile. How distinguished of him, he thought, to bow out so maturely rather than to argue stubbornly. He was learning about life.

"Raul said you've dropped out of high school."

"Yeah."

"And your parents don't mind?"

"Oh no."

"Are they going to support you?"

"For a while. I'm hoping to make some money."

"You're gonna get a job?"

The novel. Should he discuss the novel? "Yeah, I guess so." From his response, Joan obviously thought he was going nowhere, but he preferred that to being ridiculed for writing.

She got up. "Let's go back to the party."

Richard was dismayed. He thought she was enjoying this chat, and the unreal assurance of her admiration changed to real assurance of her dislike. The loneliness pressed in on him again. What was just a fit of alienation due to the grass was really the burden of his life, unshakable and remorseless.

"Are you worried about going in there?" she asked.

He could confess everything, maybe she'd take pity on him. He looked straight at her and waited for the words.

"I mean they're all nice people," she said.

"The grass has made me feel weird. So I think I'll go."

"All right," she said with what might have been regret.

CHAPTER THREE

Richard was spending the night with an old friend from Cabot, Bill, who had also invited a thin blond young man named Frank. It had all been arranged so there was no need for discussion. They seemed much like three clean-cut little boys: dressed in their pajamas, surrounded by Bill's posters and records. *Playboy* magazines, schoolbooks, and two cots cluttered the room but added to the camp atmosphere. Each had taken a shower. Frank returned from his and found Richard and Bill lying on the cots and looking at the *Playboy* magazines. They put them aside and Bill picked up a pack of cards while Richard patted a place next to him for Frank. Frank sat down and looked at the five cards Bill had dealt him. Richard had a pair of tens and asked for three more cards. Frank got one and Bill pulled two for himself. Richard laughed and said, "I wish it was for money. Trip tens."

Neither Bill nor Frank had better, so they took off their tops. Frank's chest was hairless, his nipples very pink, but Richard got a glimpse of blond underarm hair which pleased him. Bill enjoyed the look of Frank's smooth skin and flat belly. Richard dealt the next hand unsteadily, his tingling self-conscious penis eager that Frank should lose. Bill was also pleased when Frank looked sadly at his cards. Bill won and Richard quickly took his top off, fearful of missing Frank disrobing. Richard's penis strained away from him as Frank stood in the agreed spot for important unveilings.

Frank's erection pointed straight to his navel, falling forward and pointing ludicrously at the ceiling when he dropped his bottoms. Waves of longing and heat passed through Richard's body, and he painfully stopped himself from coming, slowing his pace. Frank held his penis to his belly as he turned to show them his delicious small pink ass.

Richard won the next hand, distracted by Frank's moist pubic hair. Bill removed his bottoms, but now the beautiful part was coming. Bill dimmed the lights and Frank stood woozily while Bill held his member with great warmth and tenderness, tenderness—Richard moved his lips over Frank's, moistening them as he squeezed Frank's tight superb ass. Bill in great heat was calling for Richard's penis as he removed Richard's bottoms held his demanding warm oh warm penis. Frank was putting was putting him on the bed with a hermaphrodyte's love. Yes fragile womanish man. Bill kissed him kissed him and Frank closed his warm mouth over—

The three jerks his distended penis gave were regarded coldly by Richard, annoyed that he had ejaculated high on his chest and on his belly in great quantity. He grimaced as he pulled the bed sheet up and tried to wipe the semen off. He flipped the sheet away from him and turned on his stomach to dry thoroughly. The windows were resplendent with the morning sun. He had decided to let his imagination go and Christ! did it ever. Oh, how he had enjoyed it! No, there could be no doubt—he was homosexual. And why not if it's that good?

While masturbating, his nudity had seemed lusty and exciting, but now, as he dressed, he was disgusted by the flattened, damp hairs that ran from his navel to his groin. He showered and brushed his teeth, enjoying it more than usual, and spat with vehemence.

The apartment was quiet, his mother off at work, his father locked away in his study. The kitchen was brilliant from the sun, and, engulfed by this cheerful light, he felt strong and healthy. He made eggs, bacon, toast, and fresh coffee—an unusually large breakfast. He read the *Times* from cover to cover and found it remarkably interesting. When finished, he energetically cleaned up and went to his room. He made the bed, glad to have removed any traces of his sexuality from sight.

Finally it became impossible to avoid thinking about his fantasy. He tried to stop himself from revoking his earlier judgment that he was homosexual. He wanted the issue decided and forgotten. But a voice argued convincingly that nothing had been proved: he would have to attempt sleeping with a woman before it would be. So he called Information and got Joan's number. It was eleven and she would be in school, so he worked on his novel.

He had been within a few pages of finishing for several days. Everything he had planned to write was already in it, but he despaired of finding the words to end it. He was tempted to escape the problem by killing the main character. He sat at his desk and allowed the weary sadness of the music playing on his radio to mix with the mood of the most recent paragraphs. He had one of the few moments of inspiration while working and he was finished.

The manuscript was fat and definite. He raised the papers and dropped them on his desk, listening with pleasure to the soft slap they made. He could sit back and face the problem of living now; he could enjoy life with this as his passport.

If he could use the determination it took to complete his novel and improve his life with it, then—improve his life? How cold that was! Always confined, thoughtful, and self-conscious. Rule one: be natural. Have a drink maybe and tell his father.

Aaron looked startled when his study door opened with a bang. He looked quizzically at Richard standing triumphantly in the doorway. "It's finished," Richard said. "I did it."

"Really? All done?"

His father wasn't excited and the question embarrassed Richard. He felt he had lied. "Well, you know. The first draft. But it'll just be a retyping, really."

His father maintained his serious, almost stern, look and

said, "Be sure to go over it very carefully." Aaron crossed out sentences in the air with an imaginary pen. "Thoroughly weed it out. That's very important. It's slow, annoying work, but you mustn't be impatient."

"Don't worry. I won't be unprofessional." Richard smiled ingratiatingly. He hoped to make his father be more cheerful. Aaron got up and walked over to his son with an abstracted air, putting his arm around him. "So you're all done, eh kiddo?" His father hugged Richard to his side and pulled him off balance. "It's terrific that you've finished it so fast. You know it's a terrible habit of mine to get most of it done and then prevaricate forever over the ending."

Richard laughed. "That's funny. I was thinking what a fake I am. I just wrote the ending unconsciously."

His father looked down at him, his face, it seemed to Richard, suddenly distant. It wore his father's formal mask and Richard was frightened by it: had Aaron taken his comment as a confession of amateurism? "You know what I mean," Richard continued in a rush. "I started out having an apocalyptic vision for an ending. It was almost as if I wrote the whole thing for the ending. But after a while I forgot what hideous idea I had, and in fact finished with the right thing." This speech erased his father's conventional look, but now Richard felt he was running off at the mouth about his book. He knew he had to avoid that. After all he was just a pretentious kid in the eyes of the world. His father was a respected playwright. He didn't really know if his parents believed in his book. Let him finish it, he imagined them saying, when it's turned down he'll go to school quietly.

"So how does it feel to be a writer?"

"I don't know. Am I a writer?"

Aaron exaggerated his surprise. "Sure. You know your mother and I were very casual about it but what you showed us was extraordinary." His voice had an unnatural seriousness. "I was just thinking about one of your scenes. I'm very eager to read it."

Richard thought, he's being careful to make me realize that he respects my work. "I'll give it to you now."

"Okay. But why don't we go out to lunch first?"

They both relaxed once out in the street and in the restaurant where they used to have their intimate talks. "You know, Dad," Richard said after ordering, "I always felt I was becoming an adult when you would bring me here."

"To this dump? What about when we went to Europe? That's when I felt I was showing you the world like a Henry James character."

"Well, of course, there too, but that was more exalted. There was something about not having a sandwich at home but making it into an excursion. We go into the bookstores after—"

"Admit it. That's what you liked. You'd con me into buying you all those books."

Richard laughed with him. "That's true. That's more true than you can imagine. But I was always conscious of who bought me those books."

"And that's what's led you into this disgraceful career."

Richard waited for the waitress to leave after serving their food before speaking. "It doesn't do any good to discourage me now after a lifetime of hyping Dickens, Tolstoy, et cetera. It's just a pose."

Aaron smiled and then was quickly reserved. He looked at Richard, his eyes signaling that this was serious. "You know I have made it a family joke. My complaints about writing. But it really is a terrible life. If your work wasn't so good I should discourage you." He let this sink in and then said, "That's why I hope a university will have the sense to ask you in. Because at least, if you get a teaching job eventually, then you have the money, the time to work. You're too young to have the pressure of proving yourself at this age. You're going to live a long time, I hope, and you may wish to do something other than write."

"I can always do something else, can't I?"

"You understand I'm not underestimating your talents or even your ability to use them. It's just that universities give one great freedom—"

"To freeload."

"Yes," Aaron said, laughing. "But also to investigate other things. I should still like to see you act professionally."

"If a university takes me I'll accept. I mean. Obviously. I have no desire to starve."

"You know you have to allow your father to worry about you. It's one of the pleasures of having a son."

Richard almost wept at these words. Back in his room, he reacted against this sudden sentimentality for his father. You'd think Dad was on his deathbed, he thought—as if Aaron's health precluded Richard's feeling love for him. His father's manner and conversation might have been considered routine, but it was a great change from the heavy silent disapproval of the last two years while Richard was cutting school. Richard had also lost his sullen hostility. But this soap opera bullshit, he thought, must be false. Why a miraculous resolution of their mutual dislike? Just letting him quit school solved everything. Was that possible? He felt love for his father a month after hating him. He didn't doubt that he had hated him: it seemed more likely that his love was insincere.

He stared out his window at Broadway, and New York, as it always does through windows and in movies, looked like a pleasant, well-ordered home for active, interesting people. The garbage on the streets skipped along with apparent harmlessness, and the mad old man with his bag of rags had nothing to do with Richard's life as long as he was six flights up. He loved the city from his windows but was so afraid of it on the street that he had no time to hate it. He knew this and other fears that didn't complement the writing of his book. He had to deal with them: learn to talk easily with people he didn't know; to walk New York's streets; to laugh with women and sleep with them as heartily as men ought to do such things. Fuck all that rationalizing his generation indulged in: he was going to stand over New York and challenge it like Rastignac defying Paris.

He picked up the scrap of paper with Joan's number on it, got up from the desk, and strode over to the phone. He cheered himself up with the little parody he performed: dialing the numbers so aggressively that he hurt his fingers, casually asking of the adult who answered the phone if he could speak to Joan,

35

and it was only until he had informed her of his name and she had made a polite, pleasant sound of recognition that he realized this scene couldn't end right here with a fadeout and open up again with them in bed.

There was enough of a pause to alert Joan, and she tried to help by saying that she hoped he hadn't had too terrible a time at the party.

Be honest, he thought. "I'm fucked up about parties. I get very self-conscious."

"I know what you mean."

"Anyway, I'm afraid I left a bad impression."

"No, no, I thought *we* had made a bad impression. Listen, Ann and I were going to go to the movies tonight, would you like to come along?"

Richard didn't bother to conceal his enthusiasm. "Uh, yeah, I'd love to."

"Okay. Let me arrange things with—do you care what movie we go to?"

"No, it doesn't matter."

"All right. I'll figure it out with Ann and let you know."

I'd better give her my number, he thought, but remained frozen with the phone to his ear.

"Oh!" Joan said. "You'd better give me your number."

Why is she so eager to see me again? he asked himself, once off the phone. Because of Dad? The problems multiplied with appalling speed. He had to tell his parents without awkwardness, he had to fight back the panicky feeling that Joan thought him childish for being unable to take the lead in asking her for a date, he had to figure out how to dress, how to act, how he would manage to arrange another meeting, whether he would go and come back from the movie in a cab or by subway—money! He'd forgotten that. Could he get enough from his parents? Maybe he should pay for the girls. Every moment would be a problem. Meeting them on the street—he should give them a kiss, his brother would—saying good-by. . . . Should he favor Joan with his attention or would it be smarter to play up to Ann? Maybe a little socialism was the answer, but was it possible? He laughed. He should call his brother and tell him he'd just refuted Marxism by proving there was no equality in sexual admiration.

His mind was running at an astonishing pace. Thinking that, if he called his brother and said that, it wouldn't be a chatty, funny talk. His brother would say, "Huh?" in a strained voice. Then, "That's cute," when Richard explained, and end with, "Listen I'm busy right now. We should get together soon."

What was it about Richard that his boyishness only made people more constrained? His mind was busy remembering anything that could humiliate him. Forget that, he said, nobody cares, it doesn't matter. But when he began imagining the reviews his books would get—"It is an incredible achievement. America has a new genius and should take care of him"—he was reminded that as absurd as it might be to imagine he'd ever get such praise, for all the world's giggling at youthful egotism, humanity respected fame and allowed anything for its realization. His self-consciousness would then be charming humility. How comfortable to be an eccentric author! Richard fixed his face as Rastignac would fix his—a knowing, sharp smile—and deep in this romance of ambition he hoped to forget his awkwardness.

He walked up and down in his room and stopped finally in front of his windows to look at a New York suffocating in the grayish blue of a winter afternoon. No, this preening, these chants of fame and power were unhappy. The fantasies had reality now: the world would judge this novel, and since the opinions couldn't be as good as he wished them to be, since now the growing was over, the dreams had begun to nag and not soothe.

The light was dimming, his room aging, as in his imagination he was, and he wished that fucking wasn't necessary. How sickening I am, he thought. It's the weakness that's loathsome. Other agonies are vigorous and significant. This is like being unable to walk.

He got on the IRT and found a familiar world in chaos. The subway cars reeled with sprawling names and numbers. He sat down uneasily on JOE 125, spray-painted in garish red, and stared in wonder at the address book facing him. Who was doing this? And how? The train had stopped in the middle of a tunnel and, outside a window, in royal blue, THE KING 96 mocked him with the question. How did they reach that spot?

He heard someone, in the silence of the stopped train, say with a tone of understanding, "I see your point, but I can't agree. They're disgusting, filthy people."

Richard looked in the direction of the voice and saw nothing but a silent, balding man in his sixties, dressed in a gray overcoat. The train lurched and started up, the many colored names painted on the tunnel walls pretending to be scenery. The old man shifted, a woman deep in the New York *Times* slid away from him as he moved closer. The old man had revealed SUPERDICK 107 done in baroque lettering. He looked expressively at one of the advertisements, saying, "Oh, of course you're right. You're absolutely right." Richard realized he wasn't talking to anyone, and he swung his head away from the old man. But there he caught sight of a redheaded young man dressed in a drab green jacket whose sleeves were too short and tight. He was wearing shiny black shoes and white socks. He smiled maliciously at his reflection in one of the subway's windows and, posing carefully in front of it, he brought his right arm up and flexed his muscle with great deliberation, his freckled angular face tightening with pained joy.

Richard was nervous, but having two madmen in one car was hilarious enough to cheer him up. He cautiously looked straight ahead, but hearing more tones of reasonable argument to his left, he looked past SHAFT'S LAST LAUGH 86 to the old man. He was looking right into Richard's eyes. "How can you say that? It's rude!" the old man said.

Like a clock figurine, Richard's head went right to watch the redhead triumphantly flex his muscles, left to the old man's discussion, until finally Richard lost his fear of reprisal and he got up and left the car.

For the rest of the ride and for his walk to the movie on the East Side, he adopted a new attitude. Looking down, he walked very fast, brushing past couples strolling arm in arm, knocking an outstretched hand away and not looking at the face it belonged to that asked for spare change. He slammed his shoulder into a lamppost as he veered away from a blind man with a cane and a cup rattling with coins. He was so intent on avoiding the insane that when Ann touched him on the arm to slow him up he yelled, afraid of an assault.

But what had seemed to him a loud shriek of horror had only been a gasp. "It's me," Ann said, amused. "Why were you going so fast?"

"Hi," Joan said.

Richard smiled and nodded at them. There was a line of people waiting to get into the theater and Richard noticed that they were looking. "I was thinking very intensely about something really important," Richard said, as he moved to the end of the line with Ann and Joan. "You know, like football." Well done, he thought.

"I wonder what would have happened if I hadn't seen you."

"We'll never know," Richard said. "Isn't that sad?" He was carrying this facetiousness too far, he realized. Also he hadn't kissed them and now it was too late.

"Have we got news," Ann said.

"Oh, God, Ann. I can't understand why you're so excited about it."

"About what?" Richard asked.

"Raul has run away," Ann said. She bounced on the balls of her feet. "Isn't that incredible?"

"Oh, come on," Richard said. "He didn't."

"Ann's exaggerating," Joan said with a glance of disapproval. "He left his parents, but he's obviously gone to Alec, so it doesn't make it as running away."

Richard restrained his contempt for Raul because he was afraid of offending Joan. "That's so funny. Because if my parents had insisted I go to school, I'd have done the same thing."

"Really?" Ann said. "Where would you have gone?"

"To a friend. That's why it's so funny."

Ann looked worried. "You're not kidding? You really would have run away?"

39

"Sure I would have run away. I'm glad I didn't have to, but I wasn't gonna go to school."

Joan looked at Ann with a smile of victory. "Thank God I've come across a reasonable human being."

"Why?" Richard asked. "Have people been putting Raul down for going?"

"Well," Ann said, "it's a little silly, isn't it? I mean when you were going to run away, did you plan to tell all your friends, even people who'd be likely to tell, where you were going?"

"Raul told everybody where he was going," Richard repeated, behaving as if it were a wildly funny thing to do, though he really didn't feel it was. He was torn between making fun of Raul and defending him. It was apparent that Raul was his rival, and Richard was unable to guess which attitude would win Joan. "Well," Richard said to Joan, "you must admit that's a little—well, it's not wise." Ann laughed and Richard found himself joining her. Her laughter was coarse, he thought, and his fears were confirmed when Joan looked away in irritation. Joan said, "Forget it. It's ridiculous to think about it."

Richard searched desperately for an apology that wouldn't embarrass, but the line had reached the ticket booth and it was only until they were squeezing their way to seats that Richard realized he'd forgotten to pay for the girls' tickets.

Richard became more and more unhappy while they waited for the movie to start. He looked at the seedy elegance of the East Side crowd filling the theater. He loathed them. The men who seemed to be homosexual—it annoyed him even more that they probably weren't—and the women, whose makeup was so liberal that decadence was too mild a word to damn them with. It was no relief to find young people dressed simply in dungarees and sweaters, because Richard saw in their faces a paler and more foolish bankruptcy.

They were silent while waiting, and Richard got a chance to notice how much prettier Joan was than he had remembered her being. She had put on heavy makeup for the party and it had emphasized her plain features. The low forehead, high cheekbones, and small eyes had turned her into a Mongoloid.

Without makeup, these imperfections remained, of course, but Richard was growing fond of the toughness they suggested. It was her figure that had sold him the night of the party, and now, with the dress replaced by jeans and a black leotard, he understood why Balzac had bankers lose fortunes over women. They saw *Diary of a Mad Housewife*, a movie that was both confusing and exaggerated for Richard, but apparently good for the audience and the girls. They left without saying much, Richard particularly disgusted by the press of gaudy sick people with their silly comments. Across the street there was a coffee shop and they went there.

After ordering, Joan turned excitedly to Ann. "She was really great, wasn't she? Especially in those scenes with the writer."

"I didn't like him," Ann said, with a small pout of distaste.

"Yeah," Richard said. "He was unreal." The heroine's lover, a famous young novelist, had been cast as a tall, dark, languorous young man, whose emotional aggressiveness was matched only by his sudden fits of vulnerability.

"Really?" Joan said with an inoffensive air of superiority. "He seemed quite real to me. There are men like that."

Her assurance about any type of man was stunning to Richard.

"No," Ann said. "That's a bourgeois man's idea of a man. You know, the tortured artist."

Joan looked at Ann with her eyes unpleasantly small and hard. "How do you know the director or the screen writer or anybody else connected with the movie is bourgeois?"

"It's a natural assumption," Richard said. He was pleased by the wise, bemused tone he adopted. Ann laughed and looked at him confidingly. Joan, indignant, shrugged her shoulders expressively. Richard decided he didn't care if he angered her: for some reason he suddenly felt masterful. "Come," he said to Joan. "One usually has money if one is making a film."

"I just meant their background could be working-class."

Richard laughed. "But what does that mean? Their attitude would have become bourgeois."

"Well," Joan said with a smile, "this is something between

Ann and me. She's always putting things down by calling them middle-class. Anyway, I know what she really means."

Ann covered her face with exaggerated shame. "I didn't mean anything," she said in a small voice.

"Come on, honey. You meant Raul thinks he's like that."

Richard was dismayed that Raul was so controversial, and therefore important, a subject for them. He must have clearly shown his unhappiness, because Joan, after a glance in his direction, said, "I'm glad you didn't run away also. We'd be arguing all night."

"Yes," Ann said. "You little boys are a lot of trouble."

Richard laughed. "You know, I don't think I ever recovered from the time, I guess it was in fourth grade, that a girl my age kept taunting me with the fact that girls mature more quickly than boys."

"So that's why you hang out with older women," Ann said.

"Well, isn't it supposed to reverse itself in adolescence?"

"Oy," Joan said. "You and Raul are holding us back. I mean we're eighteen. We're supposed to be marrying dentists."

Ann made a joke but Richard didn't hear it. He had assumed they were in Raul's class. There was no chance for him, theirs was only a friendly interest.

"Joan said you aren't in school. I know it's a drag to answer, but what are you going to do? Or doesn't it matter?"

"I think I'll just be a mess," Richard said, making a choked sound that was intended as a laugh.

"No," Joan said with a compassionate look. "Be serious."

"Well, if I tell you what I expect to do, you'll think I'm out of my mind."

"Oh goody," Ann said gaily. "It's really wild, huh?"

"No, it's very sedate. But I'm sure it'll strike you as an incredible pretention."

"So tell us and we'll laugh at you," Joan said.

"I've written a novel." Richard had really expected ridicule, but they questioned him closely about his book and, once encouraged, he became expansive.

They were still excited by his novel after they had eaten and paid the check—Richard, to their astonishment, picked up the checks with a forbidding look and paid for them—and as he walked them to their bus, they said he should come over tomorrow and read some of it to them. Richard was embarrassed about doing that but they insisted. Joan spotted their bus ahead and ran to catch it, but Ann turned around and kissed Richard on the cheek before running after her. As the bus pulled away they waved to him and he felt revenged on his fourth grade tormentor.

CHAPTER FOUR

Richard didn't plan to go to Joan's the next night without additional encouragement. He felt her offer could have been more polite than serious. He was unable to begin the final draft of his novel because of this anxiety. By five o'clock the issue was still unresolved, but Joan settled it by calling and asking him if he could come at eight.

Richard badgered his mother into making an early dinner, his father amused at this boyish display. Aaron had him laughing nervously through the meal with taunts about his new girl friend. His fear of missing a moment of Joan's company got him to her apartment at seven-thirty. She opened the door and they greeted each other shyly. From the foyer Richard saw two adults seated on the couch he had sat on the night of the party. Joan and he entered the living room tentatively. The male adult, a short, neatly dressed, ordinary businessman, rose and extended a hand to Richard. Joan said, "Richard, this is my father, Leonard—"

"Hello," Leonard said with a quick smile.

"—and this is Mary."

Mary, not rising, flashed a smile at Richard that seemed fake and simpering. He caught a glimpse of a dress that didn't suit her. Mary held her smile and said, "Joanie tells me your father is Aaron Goodman. I love his plays."

"Thank you," Richard said, flustered. "I mean thank you for him."

"Well," Leonard said. "We'd better be going."

Richard sat down on the couch once it was vacated and watched with great interest as Leonard instructed Joan as to what she should say if certain people called. He fetched Mary her coat, and while she was being helped on with it she said to Joan, "That's a lovely top you're wearing."

Joan received this compliment stiffly and moved toward the front door to let them out. After she closed the door behind them, Joan re-entered the living room and rolled her eyes in exasperation. "I don't like her at all," she said.

"Who is she?"

"She's my father's girl friend." Joan smiled. "Oh, I see. You don't know. My mother died when I was a child. So my father dates."

"Oh," Richard said. Her mother being dead seemed very dramatic. "How did your mother die?"

"Cancer."

"I hope I didn't upset you."

"No. She died when I was eight. It was hard for a while but it no longer bothers me." She laughed. "Too much, that is."

Richard got up from the couch and took his coat off. He folded it, laid it on the couch, and placed his novel on top of it.

"You brought it. Good," Joan said. "I hope Ann gets here soon so we can hear it."

"You can read it now, if you like."

Joan considered briefly and said, "Let's wait. Do you want something to drink or eat or anything?"

Richard asked for coffee. "Come and keep me company," Joan said, and he followed her through the foyer into a long, narrow kitchen. He sat on the countertop next to the refrigerator and dangled his legs, beating an irregular rhythm on the cabinets below. Joan, after filling a teapot with water and placing it on the stove, lit one of the burners. "Reach in the shelf behind you and get a mug," she said.

Richard did so and gave it to her while Joan got a jar of instant coffee from another cabinet. "What does your father do for a living?" Richard asked.

"He's a salesman for a toy company. Do you want two spoonfuls?"

"Uh, yes. What does a salesman do, exactly? I mean he doesn't go door to door."

"I don't know what his title is, but he handles distribution to department stores. You know."

"Has Mary been a girl friend for a long time?"

"No. He met her a few months ago." The phone rang in one of the other rooms and Joan went to answer it. She was gone for a while, and with each passing minute Richard criticized himself for his ungraceful and unsympathetic response to hearing of Joan's mother's death. It didn't occur to him that no one would take such news without a sign of being stunned. He had felt constricted after his reaction to the news. He was convinced that Joan had been offended.

The pot was whistling when Joan re-entered the kitchen. "That was Ann," she said, pouring the water. "Some cousins from California are visiting and she can't come."

Richard slid off the countertop, partly from shock. He said nothing.

Joan turned to face him and she said with a sly dimpled smile, "That isn't too much of a drag, is it?"

Richard couldn't help smiling. "Oh no." He stood there, feeling that he must say something but unable to do so.

"Milk and sugar, sir?" Joan went to the refrigerator and got a carton of milk.

"Yeah," Richard said, going over to the coffee and staring at the floating brown foam that instant coffee creates. Joan brought him the milk and sugar, and Richard fixed his drink. Joan, without speaking, left the kitchen. Now Richard was convinced that he had disgusted her.

He carried his cup gingerly into the living room and was surprised at not seeing Joan. He was deciding whether or not to search for her when she briskly entered. Joan flopped onto the couch and put a pipe and a plastic bag of marijuana on the glass table in front of the couch. "That's a good idea," Richard said, and sat in an easy chair opposite her. "Maybe it'll improve my novel."

Joan smiled distractedly while she rolled a joint. Richard watched silently and with apprehension. He might be very foolish indeed once stoned. Joan looked gleefully naughty.

They smoked two joints solemnly, as if it were a wondrous ritual, heavy with the ardor of preceding young lovers. Richard was accustomed to getting high very quickly on little grass, but he felt nothing after an amount that should have overwhelmed him. Joan stretched her legs and put her head back on the cushions until Richard lit a cigarette, and she asked him for one.

"Oh," she said while taking it from him. "Do you want to hear some music?" He said yes. She put on Otis Redding and returned to her relaxed pose on the couch. He watched her, tensing against the drug and confused by the randomness of events. When the record ended and left an oppressive silence Joan's eyes were closed. Richard got up, without thinking, and stood in front of her. What was he doing there? She stirred and he squeezed past her legs and picked up his coat and novel, tossing them to the side. He flopped awkwardly onto the couch.

Joan sat up and smiled at him. "Do you want to read the novel now?"

"Naw," Richard said, convinced she didn't mean it. "When I've rewritten it and have extra copies I'll give you one."

"I'd love to hear it. I wanted to get into the mood. But I won't push you."

"I'll confess something. As long as you're really interested—"

"I am! I really am."

"Good. Then it doesn't matter. Actually I'd rather we didn't sit around and read it tonight. All I've been doing for the past four or five months is write it. So I'd rather—" He was going to say, have some fun, but that seemed crudely sexual. "I'd rather, you know, talk. Do anything but relate to that novel." He laughed with pleasure at speaking of it casually. "I'm so bored with it."

"Not really. It must be very nice to be working on something of your own." Joan sounded as if she had led a long tragic life, deprived of self-fulfillment.

"I suppose so," Richard said with a sigh. He decided to play up the struggling writer pose. "It's hard in a lot of ways, though. You know, I mean it's good, you feel like it's something that really counts but it's tough maintaining that daily concentration. I always thought writing was a kind of ecstasy, but there's a lot of drudgery. You get that great idea and you have to hold it day after day." He had gone too far in trying to give the impression of struggle: he made it sound like pitching baseballs.

"It took you a long time to write?"

"Well, I'm not really finished yet. Probably it'll take me another month for the final draft. I guess that makes it about six months. But that's pretty fast."

"I've always wanted to do something that I could feel really expressed who I am," Joan said. She went on about the different arts she had tried, but Richard heard only isolated words. He was looking at her firm long neck and the slope down to her breasts. He would meet her eyes sharply when her words intruded, but he would be drawn down again to look at her body with mounting desire. Reality, the white cardboard walls, the bright print of the couch they were sitting on, seemed to sharpen and vibrate with threats.

I've got to kiss her, he thought, realizing that it was impossible to do. He edged his leg closer to hers so that they touched. It was a great relief to him that she didn't jump up in protest. He looked at her and she was staring into his eyes: she seemed aware of his thoughts and he felt his face collapse in dismay.

"I'm sorry," Joan said. "I forgot that you don't want to talk about the novel."

"Well," Richard said, hoping the word would allow him to rediscover the logic of their conversation. "It's just that I'm depending on it to get me out of school. I have so much invested in it that I haven't really stopped thinking about it for months." He put his arm back over her shoulders, resting it on the couch. She turned slightly to face him, and Richard found the tension of her lips being so close too great. He averted his face, saying, "You know, I'm amazed at how unlike myself I am—I mean I don't act normally with you." Richard breathed deeply and looked at her. She was beautiful.

Joan looked at Richard with knowing, pursed lips and said, "Why? I mean to be friendly."

Richard was encouraged by her expression. "You know why," he said, feeling so relaxed that he tilted his head toward hers as if to kiss her. He stopped himself, but she moved closer to him and he went on. She closed her eyes, but he did this with his eyes open, his consciousness splitting in half. He worked hard at moving his lips over hers in endearing light touches, but, despite the cold-bloodedness of his kiss, his groin tightened with pleasure. She opened her lips slightly and he wandered inside, arms tense, his head cracking with disbelief. He was kissing her!

And it lasted. He moved his hands and rubbed her back, feeling the bump of her bra strap. She didn't leap away. He heard their bodies shift on the couch as she settled into the kiss. His eyes wandered around the room casually, his penis pushed its way upward so that it made a little tent of his right pocket. He slowly moved one arm and put his hand on one of her breasts. She murmured her approval but he felt the material of her bra more than her breast; the kiss and her clothes made him restless. He was tilted toward her in an uncomfortable pose, his erection pulling away from his body so violently that he was afraid any more excitement might seriously injure him.

He leaned away from her, stopping the kiss. He kissed her throat, he bit lightly at her neck and its warmth, her body's enjoyment made her stretch out and he moved almost on top of her, his hard lump soothed by the softness of her thigh. He rubbed it furtively against her and his legs weakened, his stomach suffused with heat. This is it, he thought, and the feeling left him. He was hardly conscious of its departure while he began calculating how to get her undressed. He felt silly, almost crouched and nibbling at her neck. He could look down and see the beginnings of an inexpressible delight. He shifted uncomfortably to position his hand to unbutton her blouse.

The awkwardness of attempting to unbutton her top with one hand pressed between their bodies made Joan tense. He felt her sudden isolation and took it as an insult. He felt absurd: perched on her like a teddy bear, a Middle-Western loudmouth necking in the back seat of a convertible. Vividly embarrassing images rose like demons with mocking, distorted mouths. He pushed away from her as if bitten by a bee.

Her body was loose and relaxed, her clothes slightly crumpled, her eyes puffed and sleepy. She was there to be taken. That knowing mature person was warm and cozy, easily had. He answered her demure questioning look with the sophistication and sureness that she inspired. He leaned back on the couch, reached forward with one hand and gently stroked her hair. She smiled and closed her eyes. He took both hands now and carefully undid each button. He found every moment fantastic—incredible! It fell away with slow fluttering grace, and the awesome beauty of the fresh skin stunned him. There was a beauty mark on the rise of her left breast, and he found himself surrounding it with his mouth, his tongue touching it gingerly. The bra annoyed him almost beyond endurance, and he lifted her up to get it off. She sat up, however, and he released her, worried. But as she solemnly took off her top and reached back to unhook the bra, he felt the same giddiness in his legs, and even resting one hand on his own leg was arousing. Her bra came off abruptly, her breasts popping out like bull's-eyes: it was obscene and ludicrous. Joan looked at him with shame, and since that was incomprehensible it added to Richard's feeling of absurdity.

She timidly rested her head on his chest, and Richard knew he must have embarrassed her. He moved her away in order to kiss her lips, and that was the first genuine kiss of his life.

He lost himself in it, enjoyed its rhythm without itemizing his physical reactions, unsurprised by the feel of her warm breasts.

Joan was enjoying the embrace and she pulled up his shirt in the back, moving her hands rapturously over his skin. One hand went down and slithered inside his underpants and reached for a buttock. Richard was horrified at the image of her hands near his anus and he squirmed so as to prevent it happening without stopping the kiss. But she mistook it for pleasure and moved her hand more passionately, squeezed lightly, and allowed a fingertip to stray briefly within the crease of his ass.

He pushed away from her with a start when that happened. His erection had evaporated in a startling and disturbing manner. He wanted to rush away, but instinct had him smooth it over—he just looked at those tender nipples and baby-white skin and he was licking them with the abandon of a loving pet. He moved his hands up and down the sides of her body, lifted her arms and relished the sight: the sloping hollows of her underarms, her firm breasts, the nipples thick and hard like knobs.

He didn't know what to do with it. He was eager to get his penis in. Not only because it ached to do so, but because that was fucking and he had to prove he could do it. He unsnapped her dungarees. The act was surprisingly dramatic: the snap popped loudly and the zipper wormed down halfway.

Joan gave him yet another scare by sitting up, her face sleepy, her lips puffed and red. "Let's go into my bedroom," she said.

He expected the opposite. He heard his croaking and silly voice say, "Okay." She got up, zipped up her pants, grabbed her clothes, and tried to reach for the grass. Richard took it instead and followed her through the same hall that he had walked through in terror the night of the party. He found the business-like quality of the experience almost ridiculous. It was hard not to laugh.

They reached her room and she went in without turning on the light. She dropped her clothes on the floor and, with her back to him, took off her pants. He felt his excitement and erection with a jolt. His stomach churned with a spasm and, scared that his erection would disappear or that she would be in bed watching him undress, he hurriedly pulled off his sweat shirt, nearly falling down as he tried to unsnap his pants while kicking off his shoes. He saw her, naked, move quickly toward the bed, pull back the sheets, and get in.

He had to undress in front of her and he nearly decided to quit, but instead awkwardly took off his pants. It seemed to him his penis couldn't be erect, but it hung away from him when uncovered, swollen and forlorn. Richard had his back to her, embarrassed to turn and get into the bed with it standing at attention and equally humiliated by having his ass in view. He used his hand to pin it modestly against his belly and moved rapidly to the bed, putting his ice-cold feet under the sheets.

"You're freezing," Joan said.

Richard, the blankets up to his chin, lay on his back, his arms tense, his chilling fingertips touching his thighs. He felt the sheet on his hard penis and looked out toward the door with the soft light of the hallway spilling in. He could see himself, a boy of eight, reading on the doorsill, running back to his bed and closing his eyes at the slightest sound.

He had burned that room down.

Why? The reason was mysterious and foreboding like his present fear. The air hung over him with loathing and ridicule. He shifted to face her and then leaned over to kiss her. There was a constriction in his chest, the kind of suffocation that doing homework produced. All he felt was the pressure on his penis against the bed. Joan just lay there, one limp hand on his back. He almost felt his soul rise up from deep within him; his parched lips roughly going over hers, the whole act without enthusiasm; his heart filling with despair.

It was over. He moved away from her and lay down on his back. He couldn't do it. He felt tears welling in his eyes, just like that December morning when an older boy stole his first baseman's glove.

Suddenly he felt her touch his penis. He never had a chance to absorb the sensation, because he found himself clumsily opening her legs—they seemed to resist slightly—and putting his between them. It was like getting on a bike for the first time. He got his left in smoothly but the right one bumped against her and flopped in with an embarrassing jolt. And then there he was, his face in her breasts, his penis lying on the bed as if bowing to the altar of her cunt. He knew she didn't like this: she was tense, but he had no idea what else there was to do. Just get it in and the agony will be over.

He mechanically kissed her nipples, biting them lightly. She relaxed and enjoyed that, but to Richard it was no answer. How do I get in? He had the distinct feeling his erection was gone so he pushed forward toward that opening. He found his erection, it almost hurt on rebounding away from her, but he found no opening.

Joan's body tightened up and he was afraid she had decided not to fuck him. He had to hurry. He pushed forward—nothing, not even a hint of that moist warm place he expected. It felt as if his penis had bent backward on hitting her, so he let it rest on the inside of her thigh and hoped to discover if it was erect. It seemed to be, but, scared that it wasn't enough of a test, he grabbed it with his hand. It was elongated but not completely hard. He squeezed it several times, fascinated that it gave under pressure. He was sure that his pressure was making it more limp and he stopped. Joan was hardly breathing. She must hate me, he thought.

He put his hands on the bed and pushed off of it, scurried to his clothes, and violently pushed his legs into his pants. The swishing was loud and embarrassing.

While reaching for his sweat shirt, he heard the covers rustle. Joan switched the lamp on and Richard turned to face her. She had the blankets up to her chest. "Are you all right?" she asked, apparently without irony.

He didn't know the answer to her question. "No," he said, and covered his face while he pulled his sweat shirt on. The smell of the laundered cloth comforted him. But he felt just as lost when the world reappeared. He picked up his socks and sat down on the bed to put them on. It seemed like an act of great daring: the brilliant bit of business a great actor might devise to keep up the pretense of being normal.

Joan looked at him, her eyes still sleepy, full of trust and concern. "Are you going?" she asked.

She was a woman lying in bed, her shoulders bare, her hair

53

loose. Richard found himself leaning over and kissing her full on the lips. "I love you," he said, pulled away for a moment, and kissed her again. She murmured as he did so. His penis shifted in his pants like a bear awakening. He was depressed by that. The heaviness in his chest returned, welling in his throat.

He moved away from her. Joan's arms clung slightly to him, only hinting that they objected. "Don't freak out about it," she said. And even though it was apparent from her tone that she meant well, he was furious. He got up abruptly from the bed and began to walk out of the room, but was stopped by a sharp pain in his groin.

He stood still in the middle of the room, frightened by the ache in his legs. He moved one foot forward tentatively and almost yelped from the sensation of having one testicle strain away from his body. Was it real?

He heard the sheets rustle and saw Joan go over to her clothes. The patch of hair that formed a deep V and then the sight of her buttocks as she bent over were tantalizing. His excitement pushed his penis up even higher, and his balls felt very small and too far away. He put his hand into his pants and reached down toward them, his thighs aching, his testicles being crushed by his pants. He was tilted forward on his toes as his hand reached them. They were burning hot. He slowly pulled them up and they felt distended. It hurt. It hurt a lot. Was he really injured? It was ridiculous, he couldn't be.

"Oh, God," he groaned. His throat and eyes were teased with tears of pain and frustration and defeat, but he held them back. He couldn't face her, so despite the sharp pangs that accompanied every step, he walked out of the room. By taking very small ones he avoided most of the agony. His right hand hit the plasterboard wall of the hallway with a hollow thud as he tried to keep his balance. There were banging noises from Joan's room as if she were trying to dress in a hurry. He stopped himself from rushing out of the apartment—hoping to escape embarrassment—only by realizing how much more humiliating that would be.

But he didn't want her to see him walk in that absurd bird-like step. He braced himself and walked quickly to the living room and sat down on the couch. The muscles in his thighs and groin felt like ropes pulled taut.

"Richard," he heard her call, with even a note of desperation in the voice.

He didn't answer.

Joan came running out of the hallway in her bare feet and looked toward the door. "Hello," Richard said in a feeble voice. Her head turned to look at him. "Oh," she said. "You're here. I thought you'd left."

Somehow he didn't feel silly just sitting there and saying nothing. Only the ache in his groin concerned him. He was worn out and disgusted, too tired to care if he'd made a fool of himself.

Joan obviously didn't know what to say to him. She stood there, bewildered for a moment, and then walked over to an easy chair facing the couch. She sat with her feet curled beneath her. When she looked at him again, the hardness of her normal self had replaced the look of tenderness on her face. It seemed to Richard his own face had sagged into a disgruntled frown. He knew then it made no difference if he'd humiliated himself —he hated her anyway. "I have to go," he said.

His voice was abrupt, almost threatening. She looked away and said, "Okay," quietly. He groaned and got up, taking his novel. He was furious he had brought it. He goose-stepped to the door to disguise his pained walk. Richard stood in front of it and waited for her to let him out. But when he turned in her direction, he saw she was still sitting. He turned the lock, opened the door, and left.

He took a cab home, afraid of the train in his hobbled state. Slouched in the back, watching New York's lights pass by, he felt very small. The cab crossed Central Park: dark and motionless, it seemed like a trip through outer space. And when they finally reached Broadway and were going uptown on it, Richard looked at the people strolling the streets. Some in costumes pretending to be pimps, or junkies, or whores; others, young couples looking like they were in love, older couples looking severe. He thought they all had to be kidding. And at times he'd see them look curiously, almost mockingly, at him.

Fumbling with his money, he paid the driver and got out of the car awkwardly. The group at the twenty-four-hour grill looked at him. The wino who was trying to stay out of sight of the cop getting coffee and the cop waiting in the patrol car all seemed fascinated by Richard. He hurried into his building and reached the elevator just before it left. A few people were in it. He didn't look at them, but their presence put a tangible pressure on him. He felt his embarrassment deepening as each floor slid by. He got out with no relief, because it was early and his parents would be awake.

As he opened the door, it occurred to him that his parents weren't aware that he was supposed to have lost his virginity. That he had assumed they would know amused him enough to face them cheerfully. They were both reading in the living room, his father leaning forward eagerly, resting his elbows on his legs—a big man looking oddly like a schoolboy—his mother with manuscript papers littering the couch.

"Well," Aaron said, drawing the word out. "My boy, you're back early."

"Yes, I'm very dutiful."

"Oh ho," his father said, amused. His mother had twisted about to look at Richard. She seemed merely bewildered. He had wanted her to appreciate his comeback.

"Hi ya, Richard," she said with sudden cheer.

"I'm going to make a cup of tea, shall I make you some?" Richard felt very clever and good about himself for offering. They did take it as a charming novelty. He was thanked with pleased smiles, but they declined. He went into the kitchen and put water on. His father called in. "Did you have a good time?"

"Yes, I did."

"You took your ms., eh?"

Richard showed his head from the kitchen and drawled his words pretentiously. "Yes, I thought I'd show it about, you know, impress the rabble and all that."

"Really?" Betty said. "Somebody read it?"

He was in trouble. "Uh, yeah."

56

"So?" his father said. "Don't tell me she didn't like it?"

"Did you really go and see a girl tonight, or is that just what your father's been telling me?"

He almost blushed. "Yes, I did. I went to see Joan."

"Betty!" Aaron said. "Don't ask him embarrassing questions like that. You don't want him to think you're just a nosy Jewish mother."

"Oh sure," she said to Aaron. "I'm very worried my son, my *darling* son, is ruining himself with a tramp." They laughed. "You know," she went on, "*my* mother used to insist that all my brothers bring home their dates."

"Because she was worried they were tramps?" Richard asked, relieved to be on another subject.

Betty laughed and Aaron said, "You don't remember Mama?" Richard shook his head no and Aaron went on. "She was a marvelous woman. Betty is always acting as if she were Mrs. Portnoy, but she was really very sophisticated and very funny about her children."

"She liked you, Dad?"

"Oh, God," Betty said. "She thought he was the greatest."

The pot whistled in the kitchen. After making his tea, Richard was able to go to his room without any further questioning by his parents. He turned on the television and let it soak up the recurring, shameful memories of his love-making.

CHAPTER FIVE

The next morning at breakfast, Betty told Richard that his
sister had called, saying she was going to Europe in a week and
would stop off in New York. He asked when they planned to
move into the house in Vermont and was told in about a
month. It occurred to him later on in the afternoon, while typing the final draft, that he could go up there ahead of time and
have three weeks of pleasure with John. There was no fun to be
had in the city.

His parents agreed, provided John had no objection. When
Richard called that evening, John urged him to come, and he
decided to leave the next morning at seven. His father said,
"My God, I had no idea we were boring you that much." His
mother was quiet. Later on, Richard overheard snatches of a
conversation between them: they speculated that his date had
caused his sudden desire to leave. Before going to bed his father tried to talk him into going by plane, but Richard insisted
that he really was too scared to fly and preferred the scenery of
the bus drive anyway.

It was odd to return to his room and work on a novel about
a situation that still engulfed him: his parents retained their
sympathy for his cute problems; the trials of adolescence were

either funny or exasperating for them; he could never behave with dignity or force.

But writing had helped him. His father knew quickly that Richard was disgusted by his attempts to encourage him out of his desire to go by bus. "I'm really torturing you, eh kiddo?" Aaron said, and hugged him to his side.

"It's okay," Richard said. "You can't help yourself. But you're getting me depressed."

Aaron stood back, shocked, and opened his expression in wonder. "Why? I don't mean to."

Richard wanted to make his point without a fuss but still flash a glint of steel. "I heard you and Mom talking about my date."

"Oh no," Betty said quickly. "You can't blame us for anything you heard. That's what you get for eavesdropping."

"No, no," Richard said. "That's not what bothers me. I thought my novel was so good that you'd never dare to guess at my motivations any more." He meant them to laugh and they did—with the vigor of relief.

It took over ten hours to reach Vermont by bus, Richard nearly going mad in his eagerness to arrive. When he stepped down from the bus and saw the trio approaching, he thought they looked like a schoolchildren's book illustration of the future: John in a big, white woolen sweater, faded dungarees, and heavy rubber boots; Naomi in a gray poncho, jeans, and boots; and Nana in an amusingly scaled-down version of her father's clothes. John greeted him in his self-conscious way—a big smile with his eyes looking beyond Richard into the distance with apparent fascination. But his sister was abandoned, saying, "It's your uncle," to Nana. And then she flung her arms open and cried, "Ah, brother, to see you again is good for these ancient eyes." He hugged her and planted a kiss on a reddened, frozen cheek.

They got into the truck and John, giving Richard a mischievous look, reached under the seat and came up with a can of beer. Richard laughed and took it. Naomi, her gaiety amazing Richard, said, "John's decided to make a drunk of you. No," she went on with an apologetic glance at John, "we're celebrating your triumph."

"My triumph? What are you talking about?"

"School. You don't have to go to school. Don't tell me you're taking it for granted already."

It came as a shock. That struggle had ended with a whimper. He screamed, "That's right! I forgot. I mean I didn't realize. I won!"

They laughed together and shared his first sense of victory and release.

The five days before Naomi left were peaceful for Richard. John worked without a stop upstairs, Richard spent most of the day typing up the final draft, and Naomi took long walks, returning with her big shocked eyes, her body erect, making quick stiff movements. Richard was awed by the abstraction from life that she seemed able to achieve. He was convinced she had the soul of a poet and decided one afternoon to encourage her. He was sitting in the kitchen having a cup of tea when he spotted her coming up the long pine-covered driveway. When she came in he offered her some tea and she rubbed her hands together with excitement. "Goody," she said. "I'll make a little fire in the stove."

While he was busy making the tea, Naomi went outside to the woodbox and returned with split wood cut small to fit into the Franklin stove that had been connected into the kitchen fireplace. She poured a little kerosene onto the wood after stacking it in the stove and stood back with her face averted, tossing a match in. It went up with a roar.

"It's scary putting the kerosene in," Richard said.

"I know. But this is a badly made chimney. The wind blows the smoke back into the room. But if the fire starts quickly that doesn't happen."

It annoyed Richard that she explained it to him. He had been there the day the house filled with smoke and also the day they tried using kerosene. John had put too much of it on and two streams of flame had leaped out of the stove's drafts, nearly blinding Richard. Even though he had lived with her in the country she was still expounding on it, apparently thinking him ignorant. "So are you almost done?" she asked as he put her cup down.

"No, I'm only half done. It's exhausting typing it up. Going over it is fun, but I'm such a lousy typer that I'm forever erasing, typing over." Silence fell as Naomi put milk and sugar in her tea. She stirred the cup and stared at the stove. Richard was used to conversations ending abruptly with her. For Naomi, it was not merely a mood that caused it, it was an ideology. She had often pointed out to Richard that a group of people in a room didn't simply dislike silence, they were terrified of it. Whenever they discussed Samuel Beckett she extolled and impressed on him the significance of silence in his work and its healing aspects.

"Naomi. Do you keep a notebook like you used to?" Her contempt for meaningless talk made him ask in a formal tone.

She looked at him distantly with a quizzical tilt of her head. "When I was a kid," Richard added, "you were always writing something. You'd write poems and—"

"Yes, in my heyday. In my"—she paused dramatically—"youth!" Richard laughed. She charmed him when in this mood. "That's all in the past," she said. "We must not cling to it. Move on."

"No, seriously. Do you really feel that way about it?"

Naomi looked at him with what was almost annoyance. "What are you talking about?"

"I mean when I was a kid I always thought you were going to write."

"You know, there are other ways of living." Her eyes twinkled at him with a mixture of sarcasm and contempt. He didn't understand what was going on and looked at her stupidly. "I'm very happy the way I am," she went on with less sharpness.

"I'm sure you are. I wasn't saying you weren't. Have I insulted you in some way?"

"No, no," she protested. "I write some things. But just for myself."

He said no more and she was also quiet. He felt as if he had been crass and foolish, though he didn't know why. The conversation depressed him, and he was sullen for the rest of the

61

afternoon, saying nothing during dinner. He watched Naomi's movements and found them ugly and unbearable. They were sitting having coffee and ice cream when John said to him, "You worked today?"

"Yeah, I did ten pages."

"You're really rollin'." Richard managed a half-hearted smile in response. John looked at him with pleasure and pride. "Did Aaron and Betty say anything about getting it published?"

"Well, Mom said that she thought it was publishable, but that you can't predict it."

"Oh, I'm sure they'll publish it," Naomi said.

Richard couldn't believe that they would. He realized that, sitting in the kitchen, his head in his hands, staring at the wooden floors. It was an appalling plan: he must be mad to bank his life on it. "Even if they do publish it, that may not be enough. I mean, you know, I'll get fifteen hundred dollars and it's over."

Naomi looked at him with pity. "Richard, people live their whole lives without enough money. Particularly writers." She looked at him and was greeted by a blank stare. "Right? Isn't that true?"

They both looked at him, their eyes and posture saying, don't you see your dreams aren't real? They were taking him for a fool. "I'm not settling for that, if you don't mind."

Naomi stiffened. "Settling!" It was incredible to Richard that she was so self-righteous about his life. "I'm not talking about settling!" She spoke the words with contempt. "That's life. There's nothing to settle for."

"Oh boy," John said.

"Oh yeah, we're all losers just like you, Naomi. We should all admit defeat, so you'll feel comfortable." Her expression changed rapidly from assured anger to bewilderment. "Fuck that bullshit. I'm not just entertaining myself, just deluding myself and everybody else." He reached the instant that every argument contained: it would be dangerous to go on. And though he made the conscious internal statement that he would smash her, his rage was really uncontrollable. "Yeah, go ahead and let Richard play with his typewriter so he'll feel good. Poor boy, he can't be in mystical contact with defeat like you." He yelled it in a deep throaty voice. Naomi had risen from the table as if burned. She was trembling.

"Okay, okay, Richard," she screamed to silence him. "I don't know what's going on." Her voice was breaking as tears welled in her eyes. "You're talking like I don't care about your writing. And I do! That's what I was trying—" She began to cry. "Oh, you're crazy! Everybody's crazy!" She walked out. Richard looked at John sheepishly as they listened to her bare feet bang on the floor. Her door squealed open and slammed shut in such a way that Richard couldn't suppress a laugh. He felt ashamed that he had laughed when he looked at John. John apparently was more concerned about this fight than any of the others. He got up and listened. They heard Naomi complain loudly of humanity and then burst into tears. John went to their room.

Richard didn't want to hear their conversation so he went outside. He felt drowned by the remorse and shame that flooded his heart. It bored him: he always got into fights like this one and felt so horrified afterwards that he withdrew all his points in order to be loved again. He looked up at the awesome sky, sprayed with the unreal light of the stars, and tried to be comforted by them. How proud he would have been if his feelings had been transported into an ecstasy by Nature.

But no, he just felt cold and angry that he had run out of the house. So he braced himself and returned, but they were both still inside their room, and he ended up eating six pieces of toast and butter while reading *The New Yorker*.

Richard woke up late and found the kitchen deserted. He had coffee and went to work. The dreary job of reworking and retyping his novel was more interesting than usual. He felt vigorous and important, more confident that it would be published. Also he felt no weakness about his argument with Naomi. He understood that it meant something to him not to be cowed by her dislike for egotism: it kept him going and how could he question his mechanisms for survival?

He was humming cheerfully when Naomi came into his

room. She stood solemnly, her eyes puffed. He knew what her attitude would be—stern apology. "Hi, Naomi," he said in a soft voice.

"I just wanted to say I'm sorry we got into that fight."

"Me too."

"And I wanted to make sure, and I don't want to get into a fight now, that you understand I wasn't saying—"

"Anything against my writing." She searched his face but it was cool and unchallenging. "I understand that."

"Well," she said with what was almost anger in her voice. She looked away and stopped herself. Then she sat down in a chair and turned back toward him with a sigh. "Tell me why you got angry then?"

This was the crucial moment, because he felt the need to argue with her, to establish the difference in their perception of the world. But that gnawing desire to have it out seemed to him proof he wasn't strong enough to live by his principles without the approval of others. He had to be that strong. So let her feel there was nothing behind it but neurosis.

"Look, I was just upset. I'm under a lot of pressure."

"But I've—"

"Let me finish. You've been very supportive, you know, I mean I've realized that. You know, what can I say? I just freaked out at the idea I wasn't going to make more than fifteen hundred dollars." Naomi relaxed into a laugh that was close to weeping. Richard was overcome now with love for her and he got up tentatively. She quickly left her chair and hugged him, saying, "Okay. We're such a crazy family." She let go and they went into the kitchen. They snacked and talked the day away, and Richard felt equal and carefree with her. He was amused all day by the thought that years of honesty with Naomi had yielded less love than one lie.

Richard was made uneasy by the casual air John and Naomi affected during the drive to the airport for her flight to New York. He knew the rest of the family had deduced from hints Naomi dropped to Betty that they were on the brink of separating. Naomi had told her mother that she needed the trip to be away from John for a while. She was outraged when Betty asked if there was something wrong between them. Naomi said it was sick of people to think there was something dark and unhealthy about her wanting a few months away from marriage. She complained to Richard about the assumptions their parents and their brother were making. He agreed with her and ignored the hushed questions (as if they were in danger of being overheard on their end!) Betty or Leo would ask him over the phone. "How are Naomi and John doin', man?" Leo asked every time in a desperate whisper.

She had supported him totally about school and he returned the favor, hushing his tendency to gossip and speculate privately about his family's life. So in the car he thought furtively, "I'm not buying this calm of theirs. They're breaking up." And was immediately ashamed of even so intimate an act of treachery.

He was also disturbed by John's seriousness for the week he'd been there. All he did was work upstairs, and if the next two weeks were the same, Richard wouldn't have any fun.

He was surprised, at the gate, by the sudden show of love between the couple. They hugged in big, white woolen sweaters and faded dungarees, Nana perched in their arms, Naomi blushing like a schoolgirl. Mother and daughter went off waving and yelling good-by, Richard and John standing breathlessly watching the plane taxi, take off, and then disappear.

Richard felt very solemn, aware that John would probably be unhappy and industrious, and he didn't wish to seem insensitive and frivolous.

John wheeled about with a look of glee and said, "Well, Ricardo, let's putter."

Richard took one look at him and was amazed. "You mean we're travelin'?"

He clicked his tongue. "Do our little numerino." They walked rapidly through the airport, Richard laughing most of the way as John would slip him looks brimming with mischief.

They jumped into the truck. John turned the radio and the car on almost simultaneously. They swerved out of their parking space, and Richard couldn't contain his pleased surprise. "We're movin'! We're doin' it. And I thought you'd be bummed out."

John glanced at him, puzzled. "Why?"

Richard was embarrassed to say that he thought it would be unseemly to have a good time while one's wife was away, and at that moment it became obvious how stupid—"Do you know what I was thinking? That for some reason you weren't going to have a good time because it would be unfriendly to Naomi."

John laughed. "She's goin' to Europe man. She's not gonna be mopin'." He pointed to the glove compartment. "There are a couple of joints in there."

"Big time." Richard got them out and lit one. He dragged deeply and passed it to John. "Naomi and I really haven't been getting along."

John laughed silently to hold the smoke in. He passed the joint back to Richard and exhaled. "No shit. How come?"

"It's hard to explain." He passed the joint and began to feel its effects. The car's warmth became very important to him and he started a long investigation of its operation, pushing red and green knobs and thrusting his hands in front of the vents. He found it hard to remember which knob he had just pushed that caused an icy wind to blow on his leg. "Well," Richard said. "I've had a lot of talks with her about literary people. About Dad. You know he drove her crazy with his self-important manner. 'So and so has no ideas. He's just a reactionary shit.' You know how he talks."

They stopped at a light and John solved Richard's problem by pushing the green knobs down and the red ones up. "You wanted heat, right?" John asked.

"Farout. That's beautiful, man." Richard laughed very loudly, but looking at John reminded him of his point. "What was I saying? Oh yeah. I think Naomi decided that thinking of yourself as an artist was pretentious."

"No," John said very quietly. "I don't think so."

"I mean that's what she thinks."

"I know that. Boy, are you stoned. *She* doesn't think that."

"Oh, she does! She does!"

John let out a laugh. "Uh. Okay. Anything you say. Just don't fall out of the car."

"I know she doesn't think it consciously. But Dad's soured her on being creative. He's made her feel that writing is pretentious, because she thinks he's pretentious and she can't separate the two things."

"But she doesn't feel that way about you. She thinks it's great that you're writing." John shifted gears and looked at him inquisitively. He was obviously worried that Richard wouldn't believe in his sister's good will. And he didn't. Sure she loved him, but Richard knew that they were going different ways and he needed to prove that to John.

"I mean she's got problems with Aaron," John went on after a silence. "But, you know, I think she blanks out on certain"— he searched for the word—"phrases that remind her of him. But when you say those things she doesn't think you really mean them."

"But I do mean them!" Richard made a helpless sound. "I really do. I think it's more important to be a writer than to be a housekeeper."

"Listen, I agree with you." John looked at him and smiled. Richard saw how amused John was and he laughed. John said, "She's wacko about that."

"She thinks she's Tolstoy." They were both quiet thinking about it, and John handed back what was left of the joint. Richard bent down to smoke it, because they were in heavy traffic. The butt was so small he burned his finger but he felt the pain only dimly through the overwhelming warmth and relaxation of his body.

"Wanna do another joint?" John asked.

Richard heard himself groan in agreement. He laughed as he slowly opened the glove compartment and got out the other joint. "I'm stoned, man. Wiped out."

"You're gonna start raving any second."

"No," he protested, realizing how hard it was to co-ordinate as he was unable to strike a match and keep it lit long enough. John noticed this and smiled at him. Richard laughed and handed him the joint. John very competently managed both

67

the car and lighting the grass. Richard said, "Aren't you stoned? I don't understand how you can drive."

"I got my number goin', don't you worry."

Richard felt his face in chaos, eyes half closed, his mouth open, his cheeks sunken and lifeless. John, except for a little brightness in his eyes, seemed normal. Richard envied him. "John's totally together. It's heavy."

"Gotta keep the social graces goin'." John glanced at him, his bearded face large and cheerful. "You want more of this?" His hand held out a misshapen cigarette with a long, uneven ember trailing smoke.

"I'm goin' to sleep," Richard said, suddenly disgusted. He put his head against the seat and, smelling a mixture of the grass and the vinyl, he fell asleep to a face that was either his father or John discussing the merits of his prose.

He woke with a start when they arrived in front of the barn and he got out without responding to John's exclamation of surprise. He hurried into the house to go on sleeping but was stopped by someone saying hello. He looked up and saw Jonas, a friend of John's, who had moved to Vermont from New York to live quietly as a carpenter. His natural look of discomfort was accentuated by the suspicion with which he observed Richard. John said hello and earnestly began a conversation with him while Richard stood ten feet away, unhappy physically, and revolted by Jonas' presence. Jonas always inspired Richard's anti-Semitism, his brown, stringy hair tucked behind his ears, his pale, fleshy face slumped in perpetual complaint. When most depressed, Richard would harp on how alike they were. After a visit from Jonas, Richard would become obsessed with washing his hair and walking with greater dignity and quickness.

He was so groggy that these feelings became acute and he wanted to assault Jonas. But watching John smile and make some reference to being stoned, he woke up and wearily approached them.

"Man, you're wrecked," Jonas said to him.

"Really?" Richard asked, and looked at John. "Are my eyes

bloodshot?" He hoped to communicate to John by his glance that he had contempt for Jonas.

John said, "No. But you really popped out. Were you tired?"

Richard stretched and yawned. He was pleased by his relaxation. Somehow it made him feel superior. "No, but let's go inside. I want some coffee."

They did and Richard felt mature. Normally, he would have stood there miserably until the others made a decision. While he put out the cups, John built a fire. Jonas straddled a chair, tilting it back and forth while talking: "Hey, John, you know Ricky's mother is visiting. Crazy lady. Dig what happened, though. I go over there to help him with the chicken coop and he's taking a bath with Janey and Mrs. Harrison standing there. So he gets out of the bath and Mrs. Harrison drys him with a towel."

"What!" Richard said. "You mean his mother?"

Jonas nodded slowly. "Yep, by Gawd."

John laughed and repeated the imitation. "Buy tha sweet luv of Jeezus Chryst."

"Now wait a second," Richard said. "You mean that his mother dried him with *her* hands all over?" Jonas nodded. "And this is the same Ricky whom I've met? He's in his twenties."

John laughed. "The countryside does strange things, Richard."

Richard served the coffee while Jonas went on describing life at the Harrisons', a weird series of arguments and activities that fascinated Richard. He began to like Jonas because of the stories he told in his Brooklyn accent. Jonas talked compulsively, going on from the Harrisons to warning them that wolves had rabies and that the state cops were out to crucify longhairs. Later John took him upstairs to see his work and then Jonas left. While they were making dinner Richard tried to find out how John felt about Jonas. But apparently he had none of Richard's concerns, he just thought Jonas was a funny, disorganized man. So Richard talked through dinner and cleaning up about how Jewish Jonas was and how that didn't fit with living in Vermont and living with WASPs. He developed the

69

notion and ended up convinced Jonas was having an identity crisis and would either leave or have a breakdown.

John did nothing to keep the conversation going, and Richard was so hurt by this that, while rambling on, he had a hysterical private monologue to assure himself that it was merely John's inability to keep pace with a novelist's insights.

John had taken out the drawings for his house and was bent over them when Richard finally shut up. Richard watched him silently, afraid that he had offended him. Then John sat up and dragged on his cigarette, looking at him quizzically, "How ya doin'?" he asked with a smile.

"Uh, I'm depressed."

"Really?" John said, glancing at his drawings. Richard made a helpless gesture with his hands and nodded. "What about?" he asked and picked up a pencil, hunching over the drawings.

Richard didn't know what to say. He was embarrassed by his feelings. He thought of something that would be plausible—sex. "Well, when I was in New York I called up an old friend." John looked up with interest. "And he took me to a party." Richard stopped as he realized what he was getting into.

John got up and went toward the pantry. "What kind of a party?"

"Well, this guy is going to Performing Arts and it was just a party for those people."

John re-entered with a bottle of wine. He put it on the table and went over to the cabinets for a glass. "You want some?" he asked.

"Sure. So I met a girl there." This really interested John, and Richard regretted having mentioned it.

John had stopped in his movement toward the table. He put the glasses down and looked at him with a smile. "So did you get a little of winter's warmth?" They both laughed while John took out his pocketknife to open the bottle.

Richard was completely nonplused. He couldn't bring off a lie and the truth—what was the truth? "Well, not really," he said as it occurred to him that it was worse to say she wouldn't let him.

John had uncorked the bottle. He filled their glasses and

said, "What do you mean, not really?" Richard laughed nervously and picked up his glass, taking a long drink. "She didn't want you to?" He had sensed Richard's reluctance. John's expression of shared pleasure had changed to tactful concern.

"No!" Richard said, willing to admit anything else. "She was into it." He giggled. He saw the look of pleasure and curiosity in John's face and tried to think of a good lie.

John ran his hands through his hair and tipped his chair backward. "What's to be depressed about?"

Richard was flustered. He saw how funny it was and decided there was no escape from being foolish. He said, "I wasn't able to do it," in quick choppy words.

John seemed to fight embarrassment, but Richard couldn't be sure. John scratched his beard and cleared his throat. Richard couldn't stand that and he laughed in a high screeching tone. John's eyes suddenly focused and said, "What —what do you mean?"

He had to convince John he wasn't a schmuck. "It's hard to explain. I, uh, we had some grass and we necked for a while." Richard was almost unable to say the words. "And then she suggested we go into her room." John smiled. "So I—well, we got into bed and I had"—he laughed—"an erection. A big one."

John's smile was becoming uncontrollable. He said, "That's cool anyway. What's the problem?" They laughed and John put on a serious look afterward.

Richard imitated it. "Well, I jumped on top of her with no introduction and I couldn't get in." He said that quickly, his voice loud to bluff confidence.

John cleared his throat and dragged on his cigarette. Richard knew he'd blown it. John slowly picked up his wine and took a sip. "That's nothing. I mean, that's not—it's your first time. Stuff like that is normal." He laughed but Richard didn't. "I mean impotence isn't—"

"Impotence!" Richard was stunned. Impotence was for Tennessee Williams characters. "I don't think, uh."

"It wasn't that?"

"You mean did I lose my erection? No, I don't—I don't know." His voice cracked and he laughed helplessly.

John shook his head no and said mildly, "I didn't mean a classic case of impotence. I went through that. The first time I was scared shitless."

Richard looked at him hopefully. "Really?"

"Sure." He looked down at the drawings and brushed the back of his hand over them. "She didn't help you out?"

"No." Richard groaned. "It would've helped."

"She just lay there? Yeah, that makes it worse." John opened his knife and sharpened his pencil. "So that's what's been on your mind."

"I know. It's so humiliating that I'm in this position. I mean, I should have been fucking for years."

John laughed and looked at him with the old closeness and pleasure. That cheered Richard up. John closed his knife with a snap and said, "We should all have been fucking for years."

Richard exaggerated his laughter, hoping to be happier. "I just feel that the rest of me has outgrown being a virgin and I'm stuck, unable to become blissfully ignorant and fuck without caring." He reached for the bottle and filled his glass.

"You should get drunk and find somebody. If you're really wacko it's a mess but at least you get it done."

They were quiet. John returned to his work and Richard looked at the wine in his glass. He was half drunk already and a moment ago he wanted to be blind, but now that seemed sick and he put his glass down in disgust.

The next two weeks were as dull as Richard had feared. Even though they would be up drinking until five in the morning, Richard would always find John working upstairs. He would get up with a splitting headache at about one o'clock but John was up and around by nine-thirty. The afternoons were depressing —workmen banged all about the house putting in central heating. Richard had passed out one night, forgetting to draw the blinds, and he was appalled the following morning, when he opened his eyes into the stare of a workman outside his window. For weeks Richard would imagine what the workman had seen: the covers draped over the bedside, books and empty beer cans strewn on the floor, Richard in a thermal T shirt, black on the edges with filth, his pants still on, his head thrown back with his mouth wide open. He got up and pulled the shades down violently. After a cup of coffee, he went upstairs and told John about it. John laughed and asked Richard when he'd last taken a bath, but Richard tossed the question back at John and they laughed, agreeing it was a draw.

Nevertheless, Richard cleaned his room up, changing the sheets and airing it out. Then he took a bath. John teased him about it and his inability to hold liquor. Richard felt the jokes keenly and resented John but he never showed it since that would make him more of a fool.

Between these jokes and Richard's awareness of what he could be thinking because of his sexual confession, Richard was suspicious of John's friendship. He swore to himself every night that he would behave in an independent fashion—not get drunk and rave (as John called it) about his life. But he sat there, doing nothing while John pored over his designs, his stout muscular body perfectly still and awesome, until Richard would start talking, getting drunker and more hysterical as the night wore on. John would put away twice the quantity of liquor, unchanged but for slightly dull, reddened eyes.

His parents were coming soon and he and John were both on edge. John was uneasy about being in the house for the month it would take to finish because of the strained way the family had taken Naomi's trip. Richard couldn't stand living with them any more. John asked Richard a few days before they were due to arrive if he thought they would notice all the liquor bottles had been drained except for laughably small amounts.

Richard was surprised by that fear, but when he looked at the liquor cabinet and saw seven bottles almost emptied, he felt the constricting shame of a little boy's guilt. "Boy, that is a drag," he said.

John looked at him thoughtfully and sighed. "Well, fuck 'em."

It startled Richard to hear John speak forcefully. "Yeah. Why shouldn't you drink the liquor?"

"What is this—you? I wasn't the guy who said he was going to drink five different kinds of booze in one night."

"Us," Richard said, laughing. "I mean us. Why shouldn't we?"

John cleared his throat. "Well, seven bottles is gonna put them uptight." John yawned and scratched his beard. "You know, 'Oh, John's been drinking instead of doing his work.'"

"Oh, come on. They wouldn't say that."

John was unimpressed by his assertion. "I'm doing a lot of work pretty cheaply."

"They know that. They know it would cost them twice as much to have it done by a contractor."

"A contractor wouldn't do what I'm doing."

"Yeah, they wouldn't even get that design. Listen, when I was with them I described what you were doing. They loved it."

"Really?"

"Oh yeah. Are you kidding?" Richard nodded at him with solemn assurance. "The only thing that'll bug 'em is that it isn't finished when you promised." John made a face. "But that's because of the plumber. You told them about that."

John looked at him seriously, exhaling cigarette smoke in a thin line. "But when I wrote Aaron about the heating problem and told him it would cost another thousand, he just sent the check in an empty envelope."

"Well, it wasn't your estimate. I mean he can only be angry at Hickle for that." Richard knew that his father might very well blame John for anything if he was in a bad mood. John explained to him why it had taken him so long to get to work on the attic upstairs, and Richard's sympathies were with him. Richard assured him that his father hadn't meant anything by just enclosing a check. John seemed to feel better, but in a rush, Richard imagined how his father would look at the situation: they would be stuck in a chaotic house, the downstairs having heat put in, the upstairs being built. On top of that there would be no place to put the furniture they were moving until Hickle's men were finished. His father would be unable to write in peace.

So, just before his parents' arrival, they worked hard at cleaning things up. Richard was convinced that the beauty of John's work would reconcile them to waiting for it. The heating would be done in a few days, and surely his mother would appreciate that the rooms were neat and clean.

He was stunned by their reaction. Silently, his mother giving him significant looks, they toured the grounds with a knack for finding flaws. John had driven his truck on the lawn just before winter and deep tracks were molded into the ground. It had never occurred to Richard that this might be serious, but his father's color changed and, though John's assurance that it would be gone by summer was sufficient for Richard, his father was unimpressed. The barn wasn't in order, his father said. Richard was enraged. He said it was cleaner than when they left. Betty stopped a fight between them by saying sweetly to Richard, "You had it beautifully done during Christmas." Richard explained loudly, while his father walked away, that cutting wood for heat tended to mess things up. John seemed unaware of Betty's and Aaron's hostility. They looked at the attic and muttered something about it being nice. Richard was appalled that they could begrudge John a compliment.

The next month was suffocating. Aaron went about with a severe frown. He worked all day, was silent during meals, and read each evening without responding to questions. Betty's tone of voice had a familiar meekness to it—as if anything harder might trigger an explosion. John bluffed cheerfulness so well that Richard believed he was oblivious to his parents' behavior.

After Aaron and Betty would retire to their bedroom, Richard would go upstairs and talk with John while he painted the plasterboards he had placed between each beam. Richard repeated the stories about his father, with John glancing down from the ladder wearing a self-conscious smile. They both knew Aaron could hear him. Richard called Aaron egotistical and said that his taunting of Naomi had destroyed her self-confidence. John disagreed very mildly but Richard would insist. "You don't know some of the stuff that would go on. Like when we were in the Hamptons and she was hitchhiking across the country. You know Naomi, she hadn't shaved her legs and underarms, so when she came down to dinner after a shower he said, 'You see. A shower and a shave and you're fine.'"

John nodded his head and went on painting. Richard enumerated the times Aaron had hit him, how Leo had screamed hysterically while he was doing so. Richard's tirade shifted to his brother: how Leo had never confronted Aaron as he and Naomi had; that this had marked him for life as a compromising weakling, untrustworthy, and repellent. It was an uncontrollable vomiting that he recognized as foolish and wrong. Somewhere in the middle of his attacks on the family, he would realize that John was embarrassed and Richard would try to make it seem like a joke.

Finally John opened up. He laughed scornfully as Richard started in on his father. Richard stopped and said, "What are you laughing about?"

"Listen, it isn't so bad between you and Aaron. You should be more cool about it. You know?" He added the question softly and saw the shock on Richard's face. "Aaron's a powerful man. I respect him. He doesn't fuck around."

"That's true," Richard said with exaggerated bitterness.

"He's on my back. Not yours."

"Oh," Richard said knowingly. "So you do see that?"

"Are you serious? He's livid." John laughed, his voice rich and appealing. "He's wacko about his own life. We all are. But he lets it out and doesn't care what that means to the world. I like that. You just have to learn not to be overpowered by it."

This made Richard feel lonely. He said nothing.

John bent down to dip his brush in the paint. "He can fuck himself about this work."

Richard laughed. "He's gone totally bananas." He looked up at John working, puzzled by his words. "So you think I should just ignore him?"

"No, not ign—"

"No, I know you don't mean that. You think I should be charming and mild with him."

John smiled. "By Gawd, yessuh."

"No matter how insulting he is?"

"No, you have to defend yourself. You got to be smooth, though." John looked at him significantly. "You have to have some social graces. People are insane. You have to be calm with them."

Richard kicked a piece of wood. It sounded bleak in the hushed night. "So—" he started loudly. John hushed him. "So how do I do that?"

John got down from the ladder and put his brush carefully on the rim of the paint can. He took out a cigarette. Richard saw him hesitate. "I'm serious," Richard continued, handing him matches. "I've checked you out. You get along brilliantly with people. Is that conscious?"

"Oh, sure. I used to be just like you. I would rave and kid people until they were ready to kill me. But you can't get along like that. You have to give people room. Every time some clown says something foolish you have to smile and say, 'Really?'" John imitated himself perfectly. Richard was impressed. He had assumed that saying, "Really?" was an unconscious habit, and it was a stunning revelation to hear John mimic himself with an ironic smile. "You know," he continued, "Jonas comes along and says some wacked-out thing to me and I say, 'Really?' and he says, 'Yes' and I say, 'Big time. You're really rollin'!"

Richard forced his laughter. He shook his head from side to side in wonder. "All that stuff. You've got it checked out."

"Look, people are always showing you something they're doing and asking for your opinion. All you do is say, 'Big time. You're really rolling.'" John was looking at him with amused triumph.

"You mean when somebody asks you about your work and you sit there very still and quietly say stuff like, 'Well it was hard work but good to do, you know? I mean the reason the chimney is so powerful is because of Michel's work on it. It was really big time working with him.'"

John listened gleefully to Richard's imitation. "You got it. Gotta be humble. You have to look peaceful and humble."

Richard cackled. "You're really rolling."

"I got my wheely-deally goin'. It's my numberino."

Richard looked at John open mouthed, thrilled by knowing his inner life. He realized how maddeningly unreachable John had been. "But that's so different from Naomi's crap about honesty." John looked puzzled and Richard went on. "I mean she doesn't make the slightest attempt to relate to people."

John laughed. "She just blanks out. Naomi's in a totally different world." He became serious and stroked his beard. "She's very strong. Your whole family is strong. I mean she really amazes me. She'll get upset and challenge you on everything. With massive alertness. I mean she'll just start jumping on you with no warning."

"I know," Richard said, eager to discuss her. "She's crazy. I mean I admire her, but she goes too far."

"Well, it's hard to take but you have to remember she means no ill. You know?" He looked at Richard with careful softness.

"Yeah, I realize that. But I have to live. I can't let her run all over me."

John laughed at that and turned to move the ladder. "You shouldn't worry about that. It's my hassle."

Richard's voice was drowned out by the noise of the ladder being moved. John said, "What?" as he climbed up it. Richard repeated, "Are you bummed out by her?"

There was a long silence while John thoughtfully brushed the paint on. "Well, I really needed a break from her. You know? I mean I've wanted for a long time to be alone on the mountain. You know?"

"You mean just to—"

"Just to get up and make some coffee, watch the land, and work on the house. Without being hassled."

Richard knew what he meant. They'd discussed the magical power of working alone. Richard envied John's ability to achieve such grace.

"I wanted to do that just before she got pregnant."

"Oh. So that's why she left." He remembered her sudden visit to New York years ago. Betty had told him that Naomi might marry someone.

"Well, she wanted to go too."

Slowly Richard got the implication. "So what happened?"

John cleared his throat. He spoke casually. "She came back in like three months. You know. She had that blank look and when we were lying upstairs in the sleeping loft—it was dawn and there was a beautiful breeze—she told me. Boy, I hit the ceiling."

"You were angry?"

"Well—I freaked out. I didn't know how I felt." He stopped and Richard waited tensely. "We talked about an abortion. I knew a way of getting it done near Washington. She said she'd do it and that's when I met you."

"So that's what you were doing." Richard was uncomfortable about this story. Naomi appeared to have manipulated John which he felt was both reasonable and ridiculous. "How come she didn't have it?"

John put his brush down and looked at him. Richard thought he detected nervousness behind his quiet eyes. "Well, she never really stuck to it. All the way there we would discuss it, and finally when she was examined, they said it was too far along for them to do it. In a way that was a relief."

"Wow," Richard said, shaking his head at him. He walked aimlessly toward a darkened section of the attic. He remembered his amazement when one night he got into an argument with Naomi about eating meat and she ended up in tears over the slaughtering of cows. "She wouldn't have had an abortion."

"Yeah, that's probably true. I mean we both knew we were taking too long to get there."

Another silence. "You must have felt really trapped," Richard said finally, his tone unnatural.

John made a sarcastic noise. "Jesus. I was incredibly upset. I walked around with this bomb ready to explode. I mean it's big time having a child. You can't fuck around, you know? There's no room for being irresponsible." He gently brushed the paint on. "So I'm pleased I have a chance to be alone on the mountain."

Richard sat down and relished this moment of great drama. He felt he had the key to John's and Naomi's lives. They are weak people, he thought, stumbling into a permanent bond—Nana. It was such a classic from literature. As time went on,

John would feel trapped and decide Naomi had fooled him into having the baby; she would feel that she had wasted her life after the child had grown up; he would think that he could have lived a gutsy bachelor life. Probably John will drink more and more as he gets older, Richard said to himself. But then why am I drinking so much? The reason had to be sinister.

He sensed the onrush of revulsion before it hit. John and he were objectified in one terrible moment. Frightened little boys. Treating love and sexuality as if they were high school power games. Making fun of males drinking while Richard drained the Courvoisier. It was chic to be vulgar if you knew it was grossness.

Self-consciousness. He reached for the word and could see his brother handing it to him. Leo would sneer and say, "Wood hippies! Living their self-conscious lives."

"It's too much to deal with," Richard said aloud.

John looked at him in surprise and laughed. Richard said good night and left. It was the first time that he had ended the evening.

CHAPTER SIX

By the time John finished his work and left, Richard was resigned to the loss. He was tired of the tension between John and his parents. And the complication it created in his own relations with them couldn't be resolved.

Richard's work moved at a very fast rate and he was finished by June. His parents were impressed by the novel, but he took that for granted. They sent it to an agent, and his father wrote a cover letter that avoided absurdity. And then nothing. There was just waiting.

He didn't live well. His parents urged him to go on walks—enjoy the freshness of the country. But he made the country house into an apartment: he stayed up until five or six each morning and slept through most of the day.

It was an effort to eat a dinner that was really an early lunch. He was out of synch—his parents ended the day happily while he warmed up to the fantasies and monologues of the night. And every day began with a defeat. No mail, his mother would say. Nothing for you, kiddo, was his father's phrase. He was embarrassed by it and felt it had to end badly. Only movies finished with lucky letters that solved all.

Therefore he was excited to hear that his brother and Louise

—the woman Leo had been living with for three years—were coming up. And he wasn't displeased when his parents told him that he would have to share his room with a friend that was coming with them.

They arrived at lunch time on a brilliant sunny day. It was a shock to discover that the friend, Mark, treated him like a kid. He had become used to the assumption his family at least pretended to believe: that he was a novelist. It didn't enrage Richard. He was even ironically pleased by it and sat back listening to the conversation, feeling his own absence. He counted at least three witticisms he would not have failed to make but that went by unsaid. When lunch was over he began to notice that his brother had an unusual air of self-importance. He trailed after them as the two young men toured the grounds, and Richard's tolerance was strained by the fact that the only question asked of him was what the local school had been like when he went there. He labored at his answer and told an anecdote they enjoyed. But that was all. Literary and political subjects were discussed as if they were talking about sexual intercourse and he was eight years old.

In the evening it was the same. But when Richard woke up in the morning and found that Mark was up, he washed quickly so as not to miss the large morning breakfast. His parents weren't there. He might have known that by sound alone: *Magical Mystery Tour* was being played on the hi-fi. Leo and Mark sat with their legs crossed, their knees resting against the edge of the butcher-block table. They were smoking, and the sun caught the smoke and danced with it over their heads.

"Hi, man," his brother said with such good humor that Richard felt happy. Mark nodded at him and then he heard Louise say his name ominously. "Richard, if you want eggs here's the pan. But Betty says that it shouldn't be washed and left to dry because it—"

"Rusts," Richard said with faint contempt.

Leo laughed.

"Oh, you know," Louise said quickly. "How silly of me—you are the strange young man who lives here." She picked up the coffeepot and shook it. "There's coffee. But I think little Leo has eaten all de bacon."

Richard knew he'd made her nervous and he felt bad. He and Louise had always gotten along very well. He put a hand on her arm to add to the reassurance of his words. "Thank you. Your preparations are thorough and, I feel, vital to the health of our community." She and Leo laughed. They had always based their relationship with him on this kind of banter. Mark looked a little bewildered by the exchange, and Richard thought to himself, Oh, he's going to be surprised every time I show intelligence. Louise announced that she was going out to read on the lawn and she left. Richard fried two eggs while Leo and Mark rustled the front and back sections of the New York Times.

He broke both yolks when flipping them over and he told them about it proudly. Leo enjoyed his mood but Mark was stubbornly unresponsive. "So where are Mom and Dad that this rock-and-roll orgy is going on?"

Leo looked at him with ferocious appreciation. "You're so Proustian today, man. It's intense."

"Proustian?" That seemed wrong.

"Uh, they're in town shopping. Listen. Are the three records you have in there all you've got?"

"There's this and Their Satanic Majesty's Request."

Leo made a face. "That's not a good one of theirs."

"I am humbled." Leo laughed again and Richard was tempted to give up any seriousness. "This is a very bleak aspect of my life. My record collection is like a middle-aged person's idea of being hip." Even Mark got that one.

His brother and Mark went back to the newspapers and Richard felt deserted. He knew it was irrational, but he needed companionship desperately. I've got to separate my loneliness from a desire to be friendly to them. He would relax and let them make the advances.

But there were none. They left him eating his breakfast, the kitchen in a sun-filled chaos of drained orange juice glasses and dirty plates. He put away the milk and the melted butter and read about Koosman's arm problems but lost the thread of it thinking he was like a spinster: eating breakfast alone was an emotional problem.

He looked out the window at them as they talked on the lawn. His brother was tall and strong. Leo had a man's body and Richard lacked that. But his brother's long face and his eyes with their open expression always had something childish about them. Richard realized the look was gone. Leo leaned against a tree, talking, and his face was concentrated and joyless. Louise seemed harassed, even worried, as she looked at him.

I'm making it up, he thought. Drama, drama, drama. Fuck it. He got up and the chair legs scraped. The sound was loud and hollow unlike noise in the city, where every sound is met and engulfed by another. Mark, he noticed, looked a little bit like him. A moon face with small eyes and a low forehead. No, Mark's uglier, he thought. He was coarser. Broad, hairy forearms, his hair mousy and knotted.

Richard decided to go out. Opening the front door made a noise and they all turned to face it. They had abruptly stopped their conversation and they watched his progress up to them. Louise said, "Hello," with too much formality.

"Am I interrupting?"

"No, man." Leo was almost scornful of that possibility. "Anyway," he went on, "we should do that today, Mark."

Mark sat on the lawn in a half-lotus. He nodded with great deliberation, his eyes fixed on some spot in the distance.

"All right," Louise said in a rush, "so that's decided. But I have a lot of work to do, so I won't go along. Is that all right, Leo?"

"Sure, sure." He looked at Richard. "Uh, we were thinking of going to a pond near here to swim. You wanna come?"

"Swim? Well—"

"Why don't you come, man? It'll be good."

"Okay, I'll tag along, but I may not swim."

Leo seemed to disapprove but he said all right and he and Mark went in to change. Richard looked at Louise, who still seemed disproportionately tense. She was pretending to be absorbed.

He was in the back of Mark's Volkswagen half-back sedan, the sun roof and car windows open, trying to inhale cigarette smoke that was caught, right out of his mouth, by the wind, when his brother asked him, "Do you know where would be a good place to buy guns?"

"Guns?"

His brother nodded with what was supposed to be complacency, but his mouth was nervously tense like a child's before weeping.

"Well, you mean for a rifle or—"

"Yeah, a rifle. But I mean, you know, the best store for that?"

"Well, I don't know very much about it." His brother didn't hear him and he repeated it. "But I would say that Sears, whose gun department is very big, is the best."

"Sears?" Leo seemed almost offended. Mark smiled. "I don't think so, man. I was thinking more of a local store."

"You should ask around. But the only store that I've seen guns in is Ralph's Hardware, and Sears. And Sears has an enormous section."

"Let's check them out," Mark said. Leo dragged carefully on his cigarette and squinted out the window of the car. Richard saw him as if in a movie. Leo nodded yes grimly with hard-won integrity, his eyes seeing a tragic future. Something was up, Richard knew, but he also knew that he shouldn't ask. So he was not surprised when they drove past the pond they normally swam in and drove on to town. They stopped at the hardware store, and Leo told them to stay put while he browsed. Richard and Mark said nothing until Leo returned and said that it wasn't very good. "We'll go to Sears," he said, and a moment later laughed incongruously.

Richard wasn't frightened in Sears, despite the nervously breezy manner that Mark and Leo affected. He thought, They're obviously not going to rob it, so there's nothing to fear. They think it's illegal to buy guns—confusing motive with action. He trailed behind them and enjoyed looking at the gun section. It was commingled with the games section: Ping-pong, pool, tennis, baseball, football, and basketball equipment reminded him of his childhood when he often came to the sporting goods department to strengthen his resolve to black-mail his parents into buying him a new glove. But Richard was included in Leo's and Mark's paranoia enough to be anxious when a salesman approached them while Leo handled a rifle.

Richard felt he should stay away from them while they were being waited on, since his nervousness would make him appear suspicious. He noticed that after a brief moment of awk-wardness the salesman showed them various rifles with great enthusiasm. His brother was amusingly ignorant of guns—he deduced from the slight smiles that Leo's questions were greeted with—but of course the salesman took Leo for a city boy interested in hunting. Leo bought a rifle and a Puma knife, and Mark showed Richard some knives that looked as if they had rubber tips but were in fact throwing knives.

"You mean like out of a Western?" Richard asked him.

Mark nodded at him excitedly. "It's heavy."

After his purchase, Leo strode through the store carrying the rifle in its pouch and a few boxes of bullets in his other hand. Richard was both nervous and pleased by this dangerous flair of Leo's, but nobody even turned his head in the store. Out in the parking lot, Leo and Mark held a conference over the best way the gun could be concealed in his duffel bag. When they had placed clothes and books so that there was no bulge, Leo grabbed Richard by the elbow and squeezed. "You understand, of course, that Mother mustn't know anything about this?"

"*I* hardly know anything about this."

"I mean she mustn't know that I've bought a gun."

"What about Dad?"

This was apparently a close question because Leo made a face. "Let's get in the car," he said.

Leo's face continued its calculations and he didn't answer Richard until they were out on the open highway, with the wind blowing hair over Richard's face. Leo spoke loudly to top the wind's noise. "You see I have to register this with the town. The guy at the store registered it but a similar thing has to be done with the local town. Do you know who's the person who handles that?"

86

"I can't be sure but probably Mr. Snow. He's the tax man."

"I don't think it would be him, man."

He always contradicts me. "He's the guy who we register the car with and pay taxes on the house. That's his job. Town clerk."

"Well anyway, I'll need Aaron for that. 'Cause I said I was a resident and I'll need Aaron to prove it."

"Why didn't you say you were a resident of New York?"

Leo was contemptuous of that remark. He shook his head. "No, man. That would fuck everything up."

"Well, I can't advise ya unless I know what you're tryin' to do. I mean you don't have to tell me, but—"

"Yeah, yeah, that's right." He shifted so that he faced Richard. Leo lowered his voice. "See, it's not legal to have a rifle in New York."

"Are you sure?"

"I don't think that's true, Leo," Mark said.

"It *is*, man. I've checked it out. Anyway, I don't want them to know. If it's registered here they'll never get it together to find out."

"If you use it they will." Richard was horrified.

"I don't mean if I use it." Leo laughed.

"That's heavy," Mark said, laughing with him.

Leo reached out and grabbed Richard's knee. He lowered his voice and spoke out of the side of his mouth, whispering, "See, man, the pigs have been busting in lately and icing people. And then they justify it because there were guns inside."

"Oh, I get it. Okay." He smiled at Leo. "That's cool. I thought you thought you could use the gun and they wouldn't be able to trace it."

"I'll be underground when I use it." Leo said it casually, as if it were merely an obvious practical solution to an awkward problem. *He's going underground? He might.* Richard needed the correction. He was scared by Leo's seriousness, but with a sibling's inability to imagine a brother acting with independence and energy, he decided it was a bluff.

Their parents came out to greet them when they reached home. "So," Aaron said, and nodded wisely at them, "went out exploring, eh? Isn't it good, Betty, to have these strapping young fellows about—"

Betty's eyes narrowed with amusement. "Strapping!"

"—getting up first thing—"

"And leaving the dishes." Betty went off into peals of laughter and said, "Don't be silly," when Richard, abashed, apologized for his neglect.

"What are you forgiving them for, Betty? Pretty sexist behavior if you ask me."

"Look who's talking," she said to her husband, and Leo joined in, pointing his finger at Aaron and saying, "She fixed your wagon."

Aaron grabbed Louise, who was uninvolved and looked worried, and hugged her to his side. "Isn't it terrible how they treat their father?" He looked at Mark. "Oh, the poor fellow. Here I am behaving like a doting old man—"

"And you don't know what to do with yourself, right?" Betty said to Mark. She was gleeful and reminded Richard of Nana. "Let's go in the house."

Louise demurred. She had to read. Richard was disappointed that she didn't join in on one of his favorites: a family lunch. But it was dismaying after all. Leo kept Aaron and Betty busy describing good places to see, and Richard was bored by it. Leo hardly listened to their answers until he abruptly asked Aaron if he could speak to him. Aaron was surprised. He looked a little amused by it, but Betty glanced at Leo with a wide-eyed look that Richard understood to be serious worry.

Betty started a conversation with Mark that Richard couldn't listen to. He spotted Aaron and Leo on the lawn. His father's expression had taken on the grave demeanor that accompanied any treatment of equality. Richard was surprised he hadn't just laughed at Leo and returned to announce, "My dear, our son, who has been unable to make a dental appointment for six years, wants to go underground." Richard looked at Betty, somehow convinced that she must have guessed what was going on, and found her saying, "Well, you can't bring up Yevtushenko in that sense. You realize that he's practically a CIA agent." She tilted her head as she always had when softening the blow of revealing someone's ignorance. Richard saw Aaron go off toward the car and Leo return to the house.

Betty heard the car start and said to Leo as he was coming in, "Where's he going?"

Leo paused for a moment. "You really think everything around here is your business, don't you?" He walked over to her and pretended roughness. He put his hands on both sides of her head and kissed her resoundingly on the forehead.

"My God," she said when free, "I think you've scrambled my brains."

"You've completely destroyed any chance of serious conversation." Richard was pleased to have said this and it did seem to right matters.

"That's right," Betty said. "I was trying to straighten out Mark about literature and politics."

"Oh, God," Leo said. "Not that discussion."

"Isn't it awful," Betty said. She laughed. "I've been having this discussion for thirty years." She brushed the table thoughtfully. "But don't you realize that we learned how wrong it was to adopt that attitude in the Communist Party. I remember how foolish they were about Mike Gold. They broke his heart."

"I mean," Mark said. "I'm no Stalinist. I don't say that Solzhenitsyn is wrong about the Soviet Union."

"You're *not* saying that?"

"Well, I mean, in specifics, no. But the effect in the United States is to play into the hands of the pigs. It just becomes anti-Communist propaganda."

"I don't think he's so accurate," Leo said.

"Mark or Solzhenitsyn?" Richard asked, but nobody enjoyed the remark. Richard hurried on. "What isn't he accurate about?"

"Well, I mean that comic-book portrait of Stalin—"

"That is a silly part," Betty conceded.

"Is it?" Richard said. "Is it sillier than Tolstoy's portraits of Tsar Alexander or Napoleon?" Leo made a face and Richard's voice rose, cracking and hurried. "Come on. You can't tell me that any great novelist did better. Balzac on Napoleon? Or Fouché? They're all romanticized."

"That's absurd," Leo said.

"Anyway, that's not the point," Betty said, worried by an impending scene between the two brothers. "Take *One Day in the Life of Ivan Denisovich*. You don't think that's distorted?"

Leo shrugged. He looked oppressed, as if the argument was contemptible. Richard was enraged by his attitude. "I don't know," Leo said. "How can we know? But it doesn't matter because he gives no analysis of why it has happened, and the effect is—"

"Oh, Leo—" Betty said desperately.

"The effect *is* one of, on the one hand, making people feel that it is the result of socialism and, on the other hand, of being totally defeatist. He never says that there's anything that can be done about it."

"That's not true," Richard yelled, but his mother held their attention by repeating three times, "Leo, that's wrong."

Leo, aggrieved, said, "*How* is it wrong, huh?"

Again Richard started a sentence, "The whole point of *The First Circle*—"

"The ending of *The First Circle*," Betty said, nodding at Richard. "Those men decide to die in Siberia rather than go on helping Stalin's experiments."

"That's defeatist!"

"What are you talking about—" Richard talked to the ceiling. He was only glanced at and shushed like a barking dog.

"If you are going to broaden that word, which I really don't think you understand"—Betty closed her eyes and sharpened her tone when Leo groaned at this—"to include any act that involves death, then Che is defeatist."

"No, no." Leo bounced his right leg up and down nervously. "*I'm* saying it's defeatist because it's put in romantic terms. You go off passively, martyred, refusing to co-operate. That's not struggle. That's not what Che—"

"You're just being a fool." Richard was amazed he had said it. For the first time his voice was confident and unhurried. But the effect frightened him. Leo had jumped up.

"Look, I'm not going in for this. You two can just go on making up your little theories." Richard watched him leave and for a moment was sorry. His mother looked at Mark with embarrassment, but when she turned to him, he saw that she was upset.

"Now please do me a favor, Mom," Richard said. It was pouring out of him. "Don't make me feel bad. He said I was absurd. I said he was a fool."

"I'm not angry at you," she said quickly. She convinced him. "I was sorry he was so upset by it. That's all."

"Okay," he said, ready to go on, but he felt tears along with the words and that scared him into silence.

Richard was apprehensive of Leo from then on, sure that a resolution of their spat would come at dinner. But there was the usual exchange of literary gossip, followed by Leo's enthusiastic questions about gardening and the local people. Everyone had forgotten the argument—Aaron and Louise weren't aware there had been one—except for Richard.

His father, once they had settled in the living room, tried to extract information about what the Movement was doing, but Mark and Leo evaded all his questions and confirmed Richard's fear that Leo planned to join many of his friends in the underground. The prospect made him timid and uneasy. It would mean Leo's death. Eventually.

He started thinking of how he would react and found himself on the lawn surrounded by reporters, making a proud speech. He was jolted out of it by shame at such egotism. He looked around as if he had just peed. How absurd, he thought, if I'm heartless, it's no use being embarrassed.

The next day, after lunch, Mark and Leo said they were going for a walk in the woods. Richard went along. They stopped in a clearing and Leo cut off a branch to whittle. Mark produced the throwing knives and stood fifteen feet away from a young skinny pine. "If you hit it," Richard said, meaning to be friendly, "you might chop it down."

Mark smiled without taking his eyes off the tree. He held himself carefully and balanced the knife on his fingertips, gestured twice toward the tree, and finally snapped his wrist, releasing it. He missed everything.

Richard tried to suppress a laugh. But Mark took the failure well. He laughed and said, "Not very impressive."

"Try a bigger tree," Richard said, no longer awed by this revolutionary training. He looked at the knives lying on the ground and he couldn't resist a romantic act. He picked one up and, spotting a larch, he turned to face it. He had planned to prepare the throw carefully, but was too embarrassed by Mark's observation to wait. He released it without calculation.

"All right! Check it out!" Richard skipped happily toward the tree. His knife had notched a small square of bark off and remained embedded in the wood. He was surprised by the milky sap that oozed out over the tip of the blade. He couldn't pull the knife out of the tree and he called Mark over to help.

Mark pulled it out without complimenting Richard on his accuracy. Richard considered that a grave sin and it rankled all day. Mark continued throwing with little success. Richard felt an airy contempt for his lack of skill and he waited until he judged that Mark's disappointment had peaked before he threw again. The thud of the blade hitting and the vibration of the handle while it settled into the wood were perfect re-creations of the Hollywood ideal. Leo said, "Good, Richie. How are you doing it?"

"I don't know. I just keep thinking of the Buddhist thing. You know, aim without aiming." That sounded foolish, Richard thought, and his embarrassment was mixed with his pleasure at Leo's notice of his skill.

"I know," Mark said. "That's my problem. I'm too self-conscious."

"What do you mean?" Leo asked. He picked up a knife.

"You know," Richard said, glad that Mark had understood him. "It has to be a part of you. I mean that sounds silly, but. You can't worry that it's going to work. Just let it go."

"Yeah, well," Leo said, not concealing his amusement. "I mean like which end do you hold?"

A discussion of Richard's and Mark's methods removed any chance of success. For an hour they failed to land a blade in the tree and then began to miss everything, eventually losing a knife in the forest's undergrowth.

Richard was convinced by this childish and delightful adventure that Mark and Leo weren't going underground. It was just cowboy fantasies. He got to like Mark but was disturbed that Mark treated him casually. He found himself waiting eagerly to be alone with him to talk. But his stomach fluttered nervously when they were, and he was afraid that he would be unable to break the paralyzing fear of humiliation. They were in the kitchen, the rest of the house asleep, Mark reading the *Times*. Richard had a sense of déjà vu, confusing Mark with John. Was this the beginning of a neurotic cycle? He was afraid of not earning older men's respect and chased after them like a puppy. It disgusted him. I'm a latent homosexual. I have a shattered ego.

He cleared his throat and said, "Leo didn't pay much attention to it—" Mark looked up, startled. "I didn't mean to interrupt."

"No, go ahead."

"You know, in the woods. Leo didn't relate to what I was saying. About the Buddhist stuff. But you did."

"Oh yeah. That's heavy stuff. I've really been into that. Have you read Castaneda?" Richard shook his head no. "*Don Juan?*" Mark described the book, telling Richard of the giant dog that plays with Castaneda while he is on Peyote. The idea that there were gods of drugs that came to either kill or help the taker frightened Richard, because if they existed, they surely meant to kill him.

Richard learned something from Mark's description of Castaneda's books: Mark wanted to handle life with perfect control. He said that it was amazing to think of life noncompetitively. You allow things to master you rather than trying to master them. We make things difficult, he said, by putting our egos between our consciousness and our acts.

"That's really amazing that you say that," Richard responded. He was sincere in his remarks but conscious of their formality. "Because I've been worried by my egotism"—he laughed to deprecate the contradiction—"but I decided it was a strength and not a weakness."

"Egotism?" Mark's worried shifting of his eyes reminded Richard of Mark's reactions to his jokes at breakfast.

"Yeah," Richard said. "I mean I realize that sounds adolescent but I'm not doing what I used to—trying to get over my embarrassment of feeling unappreciated by emphasizing my great opinion of myself. I just don't believe in modesty. I think it's strengthening to admit that you think you're great."

Mark seemed lost. "Well, I think you should feel good about yourself."

"I don't mean just that," Richard said. "I think ambition is a vital part of great acts."

"Oh no. I think that's wrong. Geniuses aren't aware of their genius."

"Oh, come on. Balzac, when he was fixing up his first study, had a bust of Napoleon, and he stuck a piece of paper under it. He had written on it, 'What he did not achieve by the sword I shall achieve by the pen.'" Richard's enjoyment of this quote returned to him. He laughed, he realized, the way Mark ought to have. Mark's lack of appreciation made him uncomfortable. "I mean Tolstoy," Richard continued, "considered himself grand enough to start a new religion, to maintain Shakespeare was a lousy playwright. They were all like that. And I can't believe it's a coincidence."

Mark smiled with gentle contempt. "Yeah, but everybody thinks he's a genius. You're not including the thousands of people who thought so and were totally forgotten."

"I agree with that. But then you'll admit that, for a genius, their ego doesn't get in the way of their acts." Richard looked at him triumphantly.

Mark shifted in his chair and when he spoke his voice lost its tone of distance. "I think there's an organic process that a genius goes through that isn't complicated by worrying over fame."

"Look, I love geniuses as much as the next guy, but I can show you a copy of the first page of the *Père Goriot* manuscript. Balzac has a flamboyant and large title, a crossed out paragraph, and the rest is scribblings of his optimistic estimates of how much money he expected to make on it. And that's one of his most respected novels. It's a classic. Do you think Edmund Wilson is a genius?" Mark nodded reluctantly. "Well, he describes getting up late at night to read the reviews of his books. Thomas Mann called writers charlatans because of all this. But I don't think so. It's just a middle-class attitude that there's something refined and great about the personality of genius."

"All your examples are writers."

Richard was puzzled by this, but he saw that Mark considered it a clever point. "So?"

"Well—" Mark held the edge of the table with the tips of his fingers, as if balancing himself. "It really may be true of novelists, but I was thinking more of the way, say, that Che relates to life."

"Che!" Richard gestured to the ceiling scornfully. "That's ridiculous. There's no more egotistical an act—"

"Oh, that's fucked up. You can't call dying to free oppressed people an act of egotism."

"I'm not saying that!" Richard yelled. Mark looked at him with mild shock at his vehemence. "How else would one sustain oneself through guerrilla warfare not *once*, but many times, except by believing that you embody the will of mankind? It's a lovely egotism. Selfless and great."

"That's just an intellectual concept. When you're a revolutionary you understand that that's like the kind of thinking in liberal history books. Being a revolutionary isn't romantic. That's why Don Juan is so heavy. Through action you lose all sense of guilt and self-consciousness. Writing is very alienating, and I'm sure that's why egotism is an important part of it. But the opposite is true of political action." Mark's moon face was kindly though patronizing. Richard wanted to jeer at him for his pretense of being revolutionary—he couldn't hit a tree from ten paces. But Richard felt that was an unfair point. Yet he was hurt by Mark's implication that he was alienated and that Mark had somehow transcended this common fate of middle-class kids.

"Listen. Writers may be alienated, but good writing is not. I mean, despite the fact that it is a Freudian cliché, one writes to break through alienation, not to reinforce it. You have far too little respect for writing."

Mark made a sound of surprise. "That's not true."

"Oh, you think they're important, but you hate them for it." Richard was returning Mark's open, matter-of-fact manner. As he had guessed, it was effective. Mark was nonplused. "The other day you discussed them politically and my impression was that you thought they were all counterrevolutionary, and now you think they're alienated and don't have the mystical calm of revolutionaries. What writer do you think avoids these things?"

Neither of them concealed their hostility at this moment. Richard's adoption of Mark's condescending malice was provoking. Mark said, "Well, like I do think the only correct way of living is to be a revolutionary. Anything else supports the bourgeois world."

"Okay, so let's say the bourgeois world doesn't exist any more. Would you be satisfied with me just being a novelist?" Richard was amused by this turn of their discussion. His family had taught him that such utopian hypotheses were considered foolishness by political activists.

Mark was solemn about this grave matter. "You would have to do socially useful labor."

Richard was unable to dismiss Mark as a crude and silly young man because Richard was so much younger. "That's just Stalinism!" he yelled, convinced that Mark couldn't ignore the truth of that label and its implied moral judgment.

"Richard, you shouldn't react defensively to what I'm saying. Part of me really understands what you're into about writing. You know? Really. I felt the same way in college. I wanted to be another Camus—"

"How do you know what I'm into about writing? How do you know anything—"

"Well, I know you've written a novel and your family's very literary." Mark paused and Richard couldn't deny it. "If everybody felt the way your family does about society we wouldn't have to have a revolution. For me I've gone through a lot of changes about the values that like I had in college. In terms of the Vietnam War and what's happening to black people I couldn't really feel good about myself as an intellectual or an artist."

Richard listened uncritically. He was cowed. Mark was a revolutionary and along with Leo was prepared to make sacrifices to change the world. I'm just a schmucky selfish kid who masturbates. He really didn't feel good about himself.

CHAPTER SEVEN

In late August, well after Mark had left, Richard was sitting up with Leo and Louise after their parents had gone to sleep. He tried to explain his guilt about being politically inactive. "What I'm trying to say is that the only thing that seems real, I mean I have respect for demonstrations, I just mean deep down"—he smiled—"deep down I feel unless you're willing to die, to become a guerrilla like Che, that you're just bullshitting." He waved his hands at them frantically to stop any response. "I don't mean I think people are bullshitting. I mean I would think I would be bullshitting." He said quickly to Leo: "Did you see how I misused would-should?" He hoped that would alleviate his confession of naïve political feelings, but it simply made him feel precious.

Louise leaned forward and put a hand on Richard's knee. She spoke in a rush. "Don't worry about that. It's because you think life isn't going to change. I never thought, years ago, that I would be political. You don't have to feel that you're making those choices for life."

"Don't say that to him," Leo objected. He must have sensed Richard's recoil from even this careful and well-meaning patronization. "He wants to get into politics. This is a problem everybody has—"

"I didn't mean he shouldn't get into politics."

"Don't fight about it, for Christ's sake," Richard said, glad and ashamed that they took his worry seriously.

"Look, man," Leo said. "When you come to New York you'll see what things are like. And you'll probably get involved. I mean Louise is right in that you shouldn't worry about it. Thinking about that up here is a no-win situation. There's nothing you can do about it."

This pleasantly resolved the question and they went out to look at the bright, vivid sky, full of stars. As they were coming back in, Louise asked Richard what John was like when he stayed with him.

"Oh, I really love him. I mean he's incredible, you know. You've seen the upstairs. He does incredible work." She looked at him strangely, busy with thoughts that she shouldn't express. He knew she disliked John, though not the reason for it. He continued, hoping to change her opinion. "He's been very important for me throughout all that shit about school."

Leo bit his nails ferociously, his eyes not meeting Richard's. "Really? Oh, you know, Aaron and Betty said a really funny thing. Apparently when they came up here they had a lot of liquor that—"

Richard laughed. "Oh yeah, yeah. He and I drank it all. But we left a tiny, tiny amount in each bottle."

Leo laughed, but Louise shook her head from side to side, disapprovingly. She said, "Oh, how terrible," but with sympathy as if Richard had had this behavior inflicted on him.

"It was embarrassing, but it wasn't terrible. I enjoyed drinking with him." They were quiet and he went on nervously. "It's hard to get to know him. He's very—he's an actor. You know he's developed a really incredible method of dealing with people. He puts on that modesty, pretends he's not intellectual—"

"Why does he do that?" Leo's question was sharp.

"It's because he's an actor. He makes conversation a game, a study. He figures out appropriate lines in response to routine situations that normally one just stumbles through. I love that. I love pushing life, bending it out of shape."

"You know, Richard, that's just a WASP thing," Louise said

in a rush as if it was impossible to contain herself. She looked meek afterward.

"It's not a WASP thing," Richard said quietly.

"I just hope he doesn't try and leave Naomi without a penny," Leo said.

"What are you talking about!" Richard yelled while Louise said something to reprove Leo. "They're not breaking up. And even if they did, she owns the property on the mountain. It's a joint deed." This got no reply so Richard's anger subsided. "It's not a WASP thing, Louise," he repeated to her. "I mean his behavior. I have it. It comes from being self-conscious."

"You're not like that, Richard," she said sweetly. "You don't have that neurotic reaction to people."

"It's not neurotic! It just comes from being afraid—"

"That's what neurotic means—fear."

He found himself gaping at her after this release of her contempt. She felt his ignorance so strongly that, after correcting it, she tried to soften the blow by looking meekly at him. Richard perceived that and felt it as the meaner part of her insults. "I know that!" he yelled. He stopped the surge of rage and parceled it out to each word. "It's a very normal kind of neurosis, so *normal* that you have it. When you sit there at a dinner party as I've seen you do and run that little line of chatter, trying to organize people into nice feelings about black people and Latin Americans, you're doing the same dishonest *shit!*" He put all of the pain of being tactful and self-effacing into this speech of freedom. The joy of it was gone in an instant. Louise had jumped up as in a comic repetition of Leo's earlier flight and left the room.

Leo got to his feet and said, "How can you talk that way to a friend?" And he followed her out.

These experiences with his slightly older contemporaries frightened him. He was reminded of John's thesis: be humble, don't challenge people. They might dismiss John, but he escaped having to apologize for actions that were merely truthful.

The agent said his novel was unpublishable, but the writers at the university said they could probably get him in. He took this as a defeat, even though the writers said they thought it was publishable. His parents kept him going: "What a thing," Aaron said. "He's sixteen, a high school dropout, and he's depressed that a university wants him." His novel was repacked and sent off to an editor, and this got him an invitation to lunch but no sale.

Louise, whose women's group included an editor, asked for a copy to take with her to New York to show her editor friend. She had read his book, and their argument didn't lessen her admiration of it. She wrote him and said that his novel might be too subtle for editors to understand; that they might find it unbelievable, considering his age, that he knew what he had written. He thought this ridiculous, but he followed her advice and wrote a short note to accompany the manuscript:

"This novel is about the humiliation of being an adolescent. Adolescents see themselves through the eyes of others, as actors do, but without any control over the image projected for them. The main character is conscious of this, and the novel, in one sense, is a chronicle of his submitting to, and, at other times, breaking out of, the image imposed on him. His inconsistency, hysteria, and arrogance all arise from this trap: his consciousness of his place, his superiority to it, and his inability to break free of it.

"The prolonged absence of his parents and of his school exist because the usual image of fourteen-year-olds had to be shocked away by portraying him as independent of the institutions that rule his life—in a word, as he really is."

During the fall months, when he was alone again with his parents, he wrote regularly to Leo and Louise and tried hard to make up for his attack on her. They recognized his friendly intentions and pitied his situation. When his parents decided to go on a trip, Louise wrote him and said that a friend of hers had offered to put him up for a few weeks.

It was January when they left for New York, and Richard had not heard if he had been accepted by the university or by the publisher Louise had sent his novel to. He decided the note he had written for his novel was a mistake, and when he reread it he was suffused with embarrassment. They're laughing at me, he thought. The drive to New York was paranoid: he felt encased and ancient, as if he was being carried to his death.

They arrived late and Richard spent the night with his parents at the apartment of family friends. He slept uneasily on the couch in the living room and was awakened out of a tormented dream. His father's face merged with the high school teacher berating him. "It's Louise!" Aaron yelled. "They've taken it! Get on the phone." Aaron hustled him out of bed and handed him the receiver.

He listened to Louise excitedly telling him the details and tried hard to make it an enthralling and romantic moment. He *was* happier but only in the gentle way that a cool breeze gives relief. What really pleased him was the four thousand dollars they were to give him. It made him independent, it freed him from school.

His parents' friends, who had felt sorry the night before for this sweet young man obviously in trouble, were stunned. He was transformed in a moment.

Louise told him to come to her apartment. He rode on the train and began to realize the implications: he was going to be in the bookstores. He could pace down those aisles amid the idiots and geniuses and see his novel. All of the predictions that were made about his dropping out were shattered by that phone call. He didn't know how to celebrate so private, so impolite a triumph.

His happiness gathered strength with each step he took toward Leo and Louise's apartment, and he was ready to shout with joy when he rang their doorbell.

"Congratulations!" Joan said, and gave him an embarrassed kiss on the cheek. He stared at her and was doubly stunned to see Ann waving to him from the living room. Louise rushed forward and hugged him. "You must be so surprised to see Joan and Ann," she said. "Congratulations, Richard. Come in, come in."

He walked in and took off his coat, the sense of himself as a young author mixing with his shame of his sexual failure. "Hello, Ann," he said, unable to decide whether to kiss her. He pretended almost to bump into the coffee table and that avoided the problem.

"I'm going to Cuba," Ann said.

"And *I'm* quitting therapy," Joan said. They both looked delighted.

"What the hell is going on?" Richard couldn't contain his pleasure at running into Joan. "How do you know—"

"Isn't it a funny thing but Ann and Joan are in a women's group with me and when I had them over a little while ago Joan saw one of your letters and surprise, surprise." Louise settled on the couch next to him and signaled with her eyes that she was worried by the following details: "Joan has a lovely little apartment"—Joan laughed—"oh, it's tiny but very nice," Louise went on. "Anyway she's very kindly offered to put you up. I didn't mention in my letter who it was because I didn't want to scandalize your parents."

Louise communicated anxiety so well that it was obvious to Richard that Joan must have told her about that evening. He tried to laugh but ended up only baring his teeth—reminding him that they hadn't been brushed. "I don't think Mom and Dad would care—"

"Well, it's not that they would be such dinosaurs," Louise said quickly. "But you are their baby boy."

"Aw," Ann said. "How cute."

"I won't get in the way of your work," Joan said. "I even have a little desk that you can use." Joan handled herself well, Richard noticed.

"That doesn't matter," he said. "I don't have any work. Anyway, thanks. That'll be great." She seemed really pleased. "What was all that about Cuba and—"

"I'm going on the Venceremos Brigade."

"And I'm quitting therapy." The two women went off into hysterical laughter. "We just thought," Joan said, "we'd be funny insisting on you congratulating us. But it's true. I'm quitting therapy after six years."

Louise, still nervous, said, "Ann and Joan can't stay but you'll have dinner with us, won't you? And later Leo will drive you over."

"Yeah, I have to go," Joan said, getting up.

"Where to?" Richard asked.

"To my shrink." She laughed at his expression. "To tell him."

Leo shut off the car and said to Richard, "Joan's really a nice girl." His tone made it a question.

Richard agreed, but tensely, so that Leo didn't follow it up. While they took the elevator to the fourth floor, Richard's stomach yelled at him for his agreement to spend his nights at Joan's. She lived in a building much like her father's: thin white walls, the corridors covered by thick undistinguished carpets, and heavy metal doors for the apartment entrances. Richard wanted to ask Leo to stay for a while rather than leave immediately as he planned. But instead he said, "Boy, it must be a heavy rent."

"Yeah, it's a small place but she must be paying two-fifty a month." Leo rang the bell of number six. "But her father's paying for it," he whispered with too little respect to please Richard.

Joan swung the door open, music escaping from within. "*All right!*" she said, and made a big movement out of giving Leo a hand slap.

"How ya doin', sister," Leo said. He hugged her after the hand slapping. It was a thorough hug that provoked not jealousy but envy from Richard. "Hey, that's Dylan, isn't it?" Leo asked.

"Yeah." She snapped her fingers. "Check it out. It's *New Morning*."

Leo looked doubtful. "Yeah. I'm not sure I like it."

Joan disagreed cheerfully. "Oh, that's fucked up. It's beautiful."

"I'll have to listen to it more carefully." Leo hurried on to explain that he had to leave. He hugged Richard before going and said, his voice loaded with meaning, "Have a good time, huh?"

The apartment had a kitchenette, one big room, and a bathroom. The implication was immediate, even silly, considering that the largest and most beautiful piece of furniture was a mattress on the floor, covered by a white-knit spread.

Joan was in a full-length green robe that had no visible opening and was less revealing than her street clothes, but much more intimate.

He put his suitcase down—a ridiculous object, he felt—and sat in a director's chair next to a coffee table. He pretended to be tired.

"You've had some day," Joan said.

She became shy with him, he noticed. She lost the amazing assurance she displayed with others. He knew what that meant but convinced himself she was just trying not to make fun of him. He was unable to answer her. He nodded and smiled. She went over to the record player, built into a bookcase, and shut off the music.

I should just pull my pants down and get it over with. The idea was so funny that he relaxed and finally took off his overcoat. She had settled on the bed unself-consciously and he didn't allow himself any thought. She looked a little alarmed at his approach but he continued and flopped awkwardly next to her. He put an arm around her waist and was erect immediately on feeling her soft belly.

He worked hard at the kiss. It had to be thorough and passionate, he kept telling himself, and moved his head rather than permit a stagnant contact that would disgust her.

That delicious weakness hit his stomach and he was happy just to lie there kissing, but he had to move on and when he found the bump of the zipper, he pulled it down and remembered a James Bond movie in which the hero ostentatiously unzips a girl by remote control.

She hugged him closer when his hand touched her bare back and he interpreted this as a request for him to stop undressing her. He became a little frightened of her enthusiasm: she murmured loudly and pulled him on top of her. He was pissed off that their clothes were still on—the natural rhythm would have to be halted.

He made these transitions—convinced she was finding him

inadequate to being disturbed by her pleasure—without the slightest regard for their inconsistency. He didn't like being on top of her clothed. There was nothing to do. He broke the contact and started taking his clothes off. He congratulated himself on this straightforward act.

She turned the lights out, and they both hustled out of their clothes and into bed as if the apartment was unheated. They lay on their backs and Richard was paralyzed. He was furious at this reaction, and following it came shocks of hopelessness that he felt unable to break.

Joan suddenly moved over with determination. To see the line of her breasts and waist was thrilling, and he was grateful for the reassurance of her warmth. She kissed him and ran her hand lightly over his stomach and settled more into the kiss before stroking his penis with her fingertips. It jumped with pleasure, and he felt how tense he had been by the relaxation that her touch created. She ran a hand up his thigh and cupped his testicles for a moment before grabbing his penis. She squeezed and moved up and down its length. Her hand was cool and his penis inflamed: the contact framed it; everything concentrated in the organ so that his body yawned to the spot with desperate pleasure.

He wrestled her over, afraid of coming. He felt her disappointment and couldn't understand it. He had read at least five short stories in which the woman was disgusted by a man climaxing either too soon or outside the vagina.

What do I do? The question provoked terror. Make love. He just let himself go, running his hands up and down her body, kissing, and licking every part but one with his mouth. He pushed the covers off and straddled her body to get a good look at her. He was delighted. He lay on top of her and kissed deeply, intrigued by the feel of his penis amidst her pubic hairs.

He felt confident and her legs were spread: he lowered his body enough to be ready and pushed forward. The lips opened and he felt moisture but then a wall stopped him. His penis jammed against it and he backed up. He pushed hard, very hard, and hurt his penis.

What was happening?

He lay on top of her, feeling his sweat and the soft cushions her breasts made for his chest. He felt sexless, as if he had just done some push-ups.

Joan's hand reached down and he lifted a leg when she nudged it. She reached his penis and when she squeezed it he realized it wasn't erect.

"I don't understand that," he said in a whisper.

She tried to move, so he got off her. "What?" she asked. Her tone made him trust her. He said, "I guess this is impotence, huh?"

She laughed with such pleasure that he was amused. "I guess so. What happens?"

"Well, I mean everything's going along fine and suddenly"—he was laughing—"we hit a few air pockets just as I'm making my descent." It was good to laugh about it. They were quiet until she said, "You know that this usually happens because of the Oedipus complex."

He giggled nervously. "No, I didn't know that." He thought about it. "I don't understand why."

"You mean why it would make you impotent?" They were both embarrassed by the conversation. "Well, the theory goes, you want to sleep with your mother and you're too guilty about that to sleep—"

"—with anybody else." He laughed nervously. "Yeah, that makes sense."

"It does?" She was excited.

"About me?" He was appalled. "No. I think maybe I've got a cold." They laughed like drunks and Richard was dismayed that the relief was satisfying. "I don't think I've told you yet that I'm a virgin. I mean in case you didn't know." He started to laugh hysterically but was stopped by her turning and embracing him.

She didn't know and it seemed to have an effect similar to having told her he was an orphan. His penis was raw, his legs pulled taut, but holding her was comforting and the pleasure of her kisses eventually overwhelmed the aches. She pulled him on top of her and he obliged skeptically. She held his penis in front of her cunt and stroked the underside as she guided it in.

He felt the moisture and pushed, and for a moment the wall stopped him, but then he was in.

He smiled and would have shouted triumphantly except that he worried instantly that she was not enjoying his occupation. He knew, of course, what to do—and the motion in and out became a dance he tried desperately to choreograph.

He didn't breathe, as if concentration could help him better feel the act. No one had described it: the sensation of that hard long arced thing surrounded and caressed. Her lips would cling to the head of his penis as he pulled out and tickle and soothe as he pushed in. He clamped down on his teeth, involuntarily suppressing the scream of ecstasy he wanted to release. He stopped moving and rested deep inside her, fighting the tickling liquid that gathered in his penis. How long had he been in? A minute perhaps. Premature ejaculation. That sin only shmucks commit. He grabbed the pillow and made his body rigid, lying perfectly still. But he climaxed nevertheless, in four ejaculations that hurt.

Though the next few days should have kept him busy with the lunches and conferences of being published, his mind stayed on the drama with Joan. He would run back to her apartment after the day's activities and continue fucking. He slept with her several times, and as it became obvious that she was not enjoying it, he asked her why. They were in bed late at night and he was relaxed and confident of life: a published novelist who fucks.

She turned on the light and scurried out of bed. "I'm going to need a cigarette for this," she said. They laughed and she got over her constraint about their discussion by pacing up and down with mock self-importance. "Well, see, between therapy and women's liberation I've learned about, you know, what's been fucked up about the sex I've had." She looked at him seriously, measuring her effect. He felt numbed and told himself to squash any fearful reaction.

"Yeah?" He tried to look encouraging.

"Our sex has been good, but the reason I don't have an or-

gasm is because you're not relating to—you know—my clitoris."
She stopped walking and looked at him. Her eyes were curious
and tense as if waiting for an explosion.

"Okay," he said very loudly. "You'd better get ready for a
shock. I don't know what a clitoris is." He put his hands out
and made a big gesture of sheepishness.

"Really?" She seemed delighted.

"All right now, no jokes. It's not funny. It's absurd. It's
disgusting."

"Oh, don't be silly." She ran over to the bookcase. "Wait, I
can show you."

"I'm sure you can," he said, and laughed wildly. She returned happily and bounced onto the bed. She opened a magazine to an article titled, "The Myth of the Vaginal Orgasm,"
and told him to read it. Its headline was its point, that there
was no such thing, that in fact the clitoris is the source of all
sexual pleasure. "I didn't even know there was such a myth," he
said, and giggled.

"Are you kidding? It's a very heavy trip that's laid—"

"I'm sure, I'm sure. I mean, you know, I don't know anything." He looked at the enormous diagram of the vagina and
tried to figure out the location of the clitoris.

"So, um, you know what it is now?"

He had to make the experience even more absurd since he
could not understand the diagram. So she took his hand and
showed him: he had felt that small bump before and that
cheered him up a little.

The metaphor that the article had used to describe the func-
tion of the clitoris was that it was a penis. And when they
made love after this he treated it as she treated his penis. They
never coupled without first going through various systems of
massage and caressing of these centers. Despite, as Joan mentioned casually one morning, the dangers of "genital-oriented
sex."

He labored at giving her pleasure and was frightened by her
abandoned, hungry orgasms. She would ask him if he was enjoying the fucking, because of the rigid, silent climaxes he
would have. He thought he was. For the first two months of

living with Joan he would walk the streets enthusiastically: he felt the clean emptiness of sex in his body. There's nothing like losing your virginity, he told his brother, and it was true.

But he had no problem with his feeling for Joan. He wanted to live with her and they agreed to by the end of their first week together. To his amazement, this caused some difficulty. Louise didn't approve, nor did Ann; they thought he was too young. Louise worried that Joan wasn't serious and a quick affair would disturb Richard, while Ann felt it was Richard who would quickly desert Joan. He was enraged by their opinions. Joan was used to this kind of self-important advice and went off to have lunches with them, unperturbed by Louise's probing questions or Ann's analysis that Joan was refusing to grow up. She told Richard about them and was surprised by the fit he threw.

"That's just like Louise. She's a dumb jerk!" She laughed and he stared at her. "I'm serious. Do you know that because she knows I've had big fucking arguments with my father, she apologizes to me for any contact she has with him."

"Babes, you're being incoherent," Joan said.

"Look. When we were there for dinner yesterday, remember? She had a letter from my father, a perfectly normal letter. You said look how neat his handwriting is and she said, 'That! It's so uptight.' And she looked at me as if I would approve. And then when that friend of theirs asked if I would be going to Vermont during the summer in order to write, she said that I had a hard time writing when living with my parents."

"I don't remember that."

"She said it. And I don't know how she got that idea."

"You shouldn't let that bother you, sweetheart. That's the way she is about everybody she likes. She's very protective."

"Oh, come on! That's egotism. I don't understand why when people are finished having dinner they don't pay her fifty bucks for the therapy session that's thrown in."

Joan didn't like his sarcasm about Louise and he instinctively shut it off. They were having a love affair, he realized, and he followed its mood. They had breakfasts at three in the afternoon and dinner in the middle of the night. He liked the isolation they fell into and he didn't lose his secret pride in being able to fuck for months.

When they finally did go out, they went to Leo and Louise's apartment. They always seemed to have guests, most of them political people. His experience with Mark had taught him to be careful with them; he did so because he wanted their respect.

So he listened and gathered rather quickly their rules of behavior. The men never generalized about women and no one generalized about Third World people. Though Joan would occasionally joke about the absurdity that calling all females women could create—I saw two nine-year-old women skipping rope—it was a major sin to call an eighteen-year-old a girl. Relationships with men were dubious: he was terribly embarrassed one evening when an intense young woman said that she would never get into that fucked up isolated trip with a man, where you don't go out or see anyone else for months. She was a member of Joan's group and she looked at Richard when saying it. He worried about it and immediately said no whenever Joan asked him if he minded that she had to go out. He went so far as to ask her if she was seeing enough people, but he stopped that when she looked at him as if he were mad.

He watched his brother when the women talked liberation and followed his lead. So when the story was told that two women just out of college had decided to be gay and live together, he behaved as if this was great: nodding and smiling along with the others, though he couldn't figure out why Leo and Louise seemed constrained in their approval. But when he found out that one of the women, a month into the lesbian relationship, had begun vomiting whenever she went out and had developed such severe psychosomatic symptoms that she had started going to a psychiatrist, he couldn't contain a slight outburst, "That's terrible."

"Well, her father has really fucked her up," he was told, and he accepted it as fact, repressing the obvious conclusion. He forced himself to believe their interpretation.

He told himself these were necessary failures. There were so many successes. Joan, Louise, and Ann had a freedom of expression that other women lacked; they faced the world and didn't put on the coy ignorance that being chauvinized apparently produced. He had great respect for them, and since they credited the women's movement for their openness, he was careful about his attitudes toward it.

And then Mayday, the massive demonstration on Washington, was called. The talk about it was depressed: people spoke of the repressive Nixon regime and the heavy busts they expected to come down. Richard was too scared to go. He imagined the brutality others described happening to him and no amount of self-goading could overcome his terror. He expected Joan to be disgusted with him but she was just as frightened and had no intention of going. But having company didn't lessen his shame at being left in New York with the reactionaries and the apolitical young while the good and strong people were gassed and jailed.

So Richard insisted that they go to New Haven in the spring to support Black Panthers Bobby Seale and Ericka Huggins while the jury was deliberating on their case.

They were driven there by Leo and Louise, and his tension about it was dissipated by the strong feeling that they were just sightseeing. When they pulled up in the large square that faces the courthouse and Richard saw people milling around a wooden platform with a large banner saying, FREE BOBBY AND ERICKA, it seemed just like the picnic that Mao says politics isn't.

They went out and sat on the grass, people coming over to talk with Leo, everyone watching the police watching them. Richard was excited by the experience and he chatted away happily. "Look," he said, and pointed to the line of police across the street, their helmets a deep blue that reflected the sun. "I'm disappointed that there's no swelling music to accompany them."

But no one else was having fun. A friend of theirs, Salvatore, came over and said, "It's so depressing. There's nobody new here."

Louise objected and introduced Richard. Salvatore's kinky hair was a tall bush that the sun lit up. "Hi," he said, and stepped back to give a quiet gesture with his fist. "Salvatore. Panther Defense Committee. New Haven Branch." Everybody laughed. Richard couldn't get over it. It was the first time he heard the machismo that the Panthers inspired being mocked.

Richard expected someone to deliver a speech because of the continual activity on the platform, but nothing happened until he heard a cry that the jury was leaving, and suddenly swarms of people crowded the sidewalks that faced the courthouse.

He didn't understand why the sudden shock of activity had started. The police ran up and down the block, stopping traffic at both ends of the street and lining up opposite the demonstrators. A big yellow school bus had pulled up in front of the pretentious steps to the building. A moment before there was a soft breeze, the quiet broken only by occasional bursts of laughter from the relaxed picnickers. Now, in a steady exhilarating roar, a jammed mass of people waving banners were chanting, "*Free Bobby! Free Ericka!*"

Behind the barricades the police had put up to block traffic, Richard could see the respectable citizens of New Haven looking slightly bored. He couldn't understand that. The chanting was strong and real, the whole mass raising fists in unison and roaring for Bobby's and Ericka's release.

"What's going on?" he yelled at Louise in between shouts.

"We're doing this for the jury when it goes out," she said.

A group of people to their right began another chant. They named members of the jury, exhorted the blacks to support their brothers and sisters, and gave specific advice to the whites according to their professions. This caused a fuss. Leo and a few others were approached by a Panther leader, and after a brief conference they went over to that group and told them to stop. A few did but others kept it up. Then a voice boomed out over all the noise: "Listen! People! The lawyers have told us not to use the jury chant. It scares them. And it may have a bad effect." Richard turned and saw a young black woman saying this over the loudspeaker system hooked up to the platform. The chant stopped and Richard heard Salvatore say to Louise, "Those fucking YAWF people."

They had added rhythmic claps to the chants, and noise exploded into the air. Richard, his hands red and his throat sore, thought the New Haven citizens weren't bored any more.

Over this one loud voice that the chant had become, Richard heard people yelling that Bobby and Ericka were leaving. He saw a whole wing of color and noise swing by, the blue shifting with them, and run down a street to the side of the courthouse. "Stay for the jury," someone yelled. "No," yelled a woman. "There's time. They won't bring the jury out until they're gone." Richard's group was pushed forward toward the police, and he found himself running with others and for a moment he thought they would run right into the barricades.

The police seemed terrified by this shift until one young man was grabbed by a cop when he came too close to the barricade and was pushed. He hit the pavement hard and Richard felt cold and distant from the crowd, convinced that a riot was imminent. "Pigs!" Do I run? He was a foot away from the cop who had done it, and he understood from the crowd that something was going to happen. "Cool it, people!" A loudspeaker said this. "Just cool it. We're here for Bobby and Ericka." In the distance he heard people singing, "We love you, Bobby." Everyone moved on slowly, the scene suddenly calm.

The police ordered them to the other side of the street, and Richard found his friends sitting on top of cars in order to get a good view. The chant had changed to a sweet sentimental song about how much they loved Bobby and Ericka. It embarrassed him but he forced himself to sing and finally he enjoyed the song.

The doors opened and several plain-clothes cops walked out, behind them Bobby Seale, in handcuffs. "*All power to the people!*" everybody shouted. There was applause and the song and raised fists all at once, and Bobby smiled intimately at them while he ducked into the car. He returned a clenched fist awkwardly because of his manacled hands: Richard had the illusion while Bobby's car pulled out, preceded and followed by patrol cars, that Bobby was a good friend going off in triumph.

For the first time he realized Bobby might be electrocuted. The police no longer looked like foolish copies of tough movie cops: they meant to kill that sweet and graceful man.

Ericka's departure was even more emotional. And when they returned to the front of the courthouse to see the jurors off, Richard honestly joined in the rage that everyone put into their chants.

He watched the jurors as they came out. He wanted to shake them by the lapels. The frustration of knowing that they looked like hundreds of people who would complain of blacks and whose prejudices he had ignored, hurt him—it meant he had done nothing to prevent Bobby's and Ericka's deaths.

CHAPTER EIGHT

The jury was out for a week before admitting they were hopelessly deadlocked. The case was dismissed and the charges dropped. The trial had cost the state more than a million dollars and along with other Panther trials throughout the United States had become almost the sole concern of the Left.

Richard was delighted. He had hated being there (sleeping in unheated houses and eating improvised meals depressed him) except for the ritual of seeing the jury off each afternoon. And it must have had an effect, he thought. He finally had concrete respect for the Movement, but, to his amazement, they didn't give themselves credit or feel encouraged by the victory.

Two days after they returned to New York City his brother and Louise invited Richard and Joan over for dinner. The phone rang while they were having coffee and Louise announced, after a brief conversation, that Aaron was in New York and was coming over.

Joan gulped for air and Richard laughed when she exaggerated her nervousness by running to the nearest mirror and fluffing her hair. They were still joking when Richard's father arrived, and Aaron listened to Leo's telling of their hilarity with impatience.

Richard realized that Aaron was preoccupied. He hadn't even bothered to charm Joan. "What's up?" Richard asked. "What brings you to New York?"

"Well, it's over the Padilla thing. I've come in to do an article for Henry Wilson to accompany the letter Sartre and everybody else has signed to Fidel."

"It's such a big deal you have to come into New York?"

"Well, they're in a rush. They want it in this issue. And it is quite important. Whatever you may think, young man," Aaron said, his eyes telegraphing the imminent sarcastic reproach, "your father is considered to have some influence."

"What is it they want you to write?" Louise asked this question in a hushed voice. She held her head in her hands as if she were in pain.

"Uh, essentially background to their letter from the intelligentsia." Aaron smiled to take the curse off his last word. "So that people know what has happened to Padilla."

"What has happened to Padilla?" Richard asked.

"He has confessed to being a counterrevolutionary." Aaron looked blank for a moment and then laughed scornfully. "It's a terrible thing, but I can't help laughing at the idea. Poor helpless Eduardo, who can't make a cup of coffee for himself, was accused of being a CIA agent."

"By Fidel?" Leo asked.

"No, of course not. You think Fidel cares about a spoiled avant-garde poet? It's infighting on the part of the Writers Union. Fidel has been put in an untenable position by them. They're pro-Soviet and they're in the process of pushing out the real leftists in the intellectual circles. Fidel's hands are tied because he's become utterly dependent on the Soviet Union. They've had ghastly crop failures and Fidel's being pushed into taking a hard Stalinist line."

"You mean he's a patsie?" Richard asked.

"Fidel!" Aaron was shocked. "A patsie?"

"No, no," Richard hurried to explain. "Padilla."

"Oh yes. Exactly. They know this is the time to make their move. Fidel has been protecting all those elements in Cuba from Soviet pressure for years. Those old shits of the Communist Party are daring Fidel to intervene. They know he won't risk the food the Cubans need from the Soviet Union to keep the arts out of the clutches of those old CP farts."

"Are you going to say that in the article?" Louise asked. "About Soviet pressure?"

"Oh, my God, yes! I have to make that clear."

Louise leaned forward and touched Aaron on the arm. "Good. I'm glad you'll put that in, Aaron. You know, so that no one will think that Fidel is another Stalin."

"Yeah," Leo said. "And also so that it's clear that the United States is responsible."

Aaron looked at Leo, his face slightly puzzled. "You mean because of the embargo?" Leo said yes, and Aaron continued. "Well, you know it's hopeless to try to prevent people from misunderstanding and believing that this is a betrayal of Cuba. From both sides. Fidel will be outraged. I expect to be attacked by leftists. Certainly nothing will prevent reactionaries from being delighted that Sartre and the intellectual world are attacking Fidel."

"But, Aaron, don't you think you should make it clear that, at least, you are not doing that?" Louise pleaded.

"Frankly," Leo said, "I doubt the sincerity of the other people."

"What are you talking about?" Aaron didn't conceal his knowledge of what Leo meant by this statement, he merely used the words to invest his anger. "Are you talking about Sartre and the others who signed the petition?"

Richard wished that Leo would take the hint and back off, but Leo said that he did. "Are you crazy?" Aaron asked, searching the room with his eyes for support. "You can't mean that. You're talking about people who have been *active* in the left for longer than you've lived. Some of them"—and Aaron rattled off a series of Spanish names whose rhythm alone meant powerful Communism to Richard—"are responsible for the Revolution itself."

Leo made a face and twisted in his chair. "Not most of them," he said. "Not the ones who will attract American interest. All anybody is going to get out of it is that Sartre has rejected Fidel."

"Leo!" Aaron snapped the word out as if it were a command. "Don't fall into that old Communist Party bullshit."

"It doesn't matter what people will think," Richard said. They looked at him as if surprised by his existence. He felt foolish suddenly. "I mean, nothing is going to convince people who are already reactionary that Fidel jailing poets is a noble act. It's better to address reasonable people reasonably, right?"

Leo smiled with regret at having to restrain his sarcasm. "The point about being revolutionary, Richard," he said gently, "is that you try to convince people of the correctness of one's opinions."

"Yeah. But not by lying." Richard lost his timidity while Leo spoke. He smiled at Leo with unrestrained malice.

"Come on, man," Leo said, disgusted. Louise reproved him, also, saying, "You know, Richard, that Leo wouldn't suggest Aaron lie."

"The *point*," Aaron said, and waited for their attention, "is that I can't temper my judgments in anticipation of how they may be interpreted. That leads to bad writing. I shall say what I think and if that's misused, it's unfortunate but unavoidable."

Richard, of course, remembered and thought over only this aspect of his father's problem. It was obvious to him that his family had always stood for writing the truth in clear, fearless prose, and Richard was surprised that Leo and Louise even attempted to get around that maxim. From every discussion of political tactics that Richard remembered the family having, the point was made over and over: the Rosenbergs should never have attempted to conceal that they were members of the Communist Party; indeed, no one during the McCarthy period should have adopted that defensive posture, no matter how terrifying and hysterical the country's anti-Communism was. Only the Soviet Union inspired people to conceal their true ideology behind metaphors of patriotism, because they were ashamed of the mockery they had made of socialism. Richard remembered Leo arrogantly saying that movements must not blindly support other nations, that revolutionary movements depend on their own people and resources for truth and success. It was impossible for Richard to reconcile that with Leo saying Aaron shouldn't publicly criticize Fidel for wrong acts.

He walked home with Joan, pleased that his brother had stumbled and crossed into the reactionary camp. "Well," he said, with little explosions of nasty laughter, "my brother, the madcap student revolutionary, who used to ridicule the Old Left for its behaving like an old maid defending her virtue, has become a Stalinist at twenty-five. I should have thought he'd have lasted until his forties at least."

Joan didn't respond and Richard, guilty that he was enjoying this imagined score over his brother, was bothered by her silence. When they were home he said, his voice bluffing confidence, "Weren't you amazed by Leo's behavior?"

"No." She glanced at him and then walked about nervously, straightening the room.

Richard said, "I take it that you agreed with him or something."

"Richard," she said with sudden urgency. "You're feeling a little crazy about this, aren't you?"

"Huh?" He was shocked. She looked meekly and hopefully at him and he sensed that it was important to say no more on the subject.

Joan told him that night that she felt it was bad for her to live off his money and that she was going to get a part-time job. He enjoyed a brief pretense of being manly and protective but was even more thrilled by her long speech that having her own money was healthier for their relationship. After it was settled, he said, "Well, we're straight out of a New York *Times* article or something."

"What?"

"You know. Front page of the second section. YOUNG COUPLES FOUND TO REJECT OLD WAYS."

"We're not doing anything special."

"I know. I wasn't being egotistical. That's what I meant. We're right in the cultural flow."

"Don't say that. That's depressing."

"But it's true. You go off to women's meetings while I wash the dishes." What pleased him was the idea that *he* had secured love so early. He lay awake beside her telling himself he needn't accomplish anything else. The world would shortly reward him for the smarts it took to survive feminism and the gross commercialism of publishing. I live with honor, he thought, conscious only of the words' romantic glow.

Joan left the house early to look for work and Richard found himself playing over the political discussion of last night. He was filled with confident, contemptuous judgments of the political people he had met, all of whom he thought of as being summed up in his brother's person. He admitted to himself that he was disappointed in them for no other reason than the surprise of learning that they were not only no smarter than he, but just as self-indulgent and bourgeois. He felt nasty thinking it, but he refused to shut up the undisciplined, irrational criticism: kids don't make revolutions.

After the first rush of feeling superior to political people, Richard began to feel nauseous and bored. He was aware only dimly that these intense shifts of feeling about politics were due to the complications of making judgments based on his emotional ties to his family. When he noticed that his belief of the inadequacy of young movement people was accompanied by contempt and that when he *had* believed in his brother he then felt guilt and self-righteousness, he thought suddenly, I'm mimicking my father and brother. And was so appalled that he instantly decided this was examining himself too closely and could only lead to total passivity. He had to take his own judgments on faith. If they were due to others originally, that couldn't change them now.

His father's article appeared without Richard thinking anything more about it. He thought of it as a purely family matter and, when he and Joan were invited to dinner at Mark's apartment, Richard was unprepared for the question that a young woman asked him immediately after they were introduced. "Why doesn't Leo confront your father about his article?" she said aggressively, but with a charming, self-satisfied smile.

Joan had told him that Lisa, his questioner, was a lot of fun, though slightly crazy. Madness being a loosely applied term by his friends, Richard thought this meant she was frivolous, and her appearance fit that image. Lisa was small with curly ringlets that along with her oval face made her seem like a clown. "Your sentence doesn't make clear whose article you're talking about. Leo's or my father's."

"Come on," Lisa said, even more harshly but still smiling. "Leo's behaving like a whimp."

"Lisa!" Mark said reprovingly.

"It's true!" She protested. "He tells me a lot of liberal shit about how there is no point in dealing with it because it's already done. That's whimpy."

She said all this in a high voice with such delight and animation that Richard was confused by her insistence and the alarm in Mark's face. She was apparently serious. But since her appearance was easygoing, Richard felt confident. "Leo's smart not to," he said. "Dad would destroy him. Because Leo knows little or nothing about it and because Dad's right and Leo's wrong." Richard laughed at Lisa's expression of astonishment, "You didn't expect that, eh? He's being whimpy because his position is just peeved self-righteousness. Leo knows he's wrong." Richard looked at Mark and quickly felt the need to impress him. "Yes, I have the gall to agree with my father."

"That's not new," Mark said.

"I can't believe—" Lisa began but Mark interrupted: "Set the table while I check out the food."

Salvatore, who shared the large apartment with Mark and Lisa, entered the living room. Richard listened casually to Joan's conversation with Sal about the new Stones album. Lisa had put him in a contentious mood, and he wanted to tell Joan and Sal that they were fools to discuss the Stones seriously. But that was a private snobbery he knew he should never reveal to his contemporaries. He prepared himself for further harassment from Lisa while they were eating, but the talk was casual.

He was so preoccupied with imagined arguments about Aaron's article that he didn't hear Lisa's next reference to it. She was handing him what proved to be a watery cup of coffee and he smiled automatically at her friendly expression. "I'm sorry, what did you say?" Richard asked.

"I said, So you think Leo's just pretending to disapprove of Aaron's article?"

"Oh no, I never said that. I think that Leo wouldn't dare criticize Dad about it because Dad'd tear him apart."

"So you agree with your father?" Lisa asked with a prosecutor's anticipatory glee at the discovery of a weakness.

Richard couldn't answer at first, afraid of the terms it might create for a discussion. "Yeah, I do. I can't believe I'm sitting here terrified to admit it." He looked at them during the silence that followed. Suspicious of their private thoughts, he said angrily to Mark: "And I resent your crack that it's not unusual for me. I've fought with him over everything in the past few years. In fact, *inside*, it feels like he's agreeing with me, not the reverse."

"Why are you so defensive about it?" Lisa asked with that familiar tone of a person beginning to interrogate.

Richard felt clever and he smiled to show it. "Because you keep expressing your incredulity about my opinion as if you were about to drop an atomic bomb. "

Salvatore laughed while both Mark and Joan showed in their smiles an acknowledgment of the justice of Richard's remark. When attacked, nothing was more important to Richard than the approval of the bystanders.

"How do you know Padilla wasn't an agent?"

"Come on. He was accused of helping a CIA agent to develop propaganda for anti-Cuban articles published in the United States."

"He admitted!" Lisa said triumphantly. "He admitted he helped an agent."

"All right," Richard said, repeating his clever smile and making a dramatic gesture with his arm. "He admitted. Now do you really believe the CIA would bother to research such an article? Have you noticed that reactionary columnists are suddenly showing scruples about writing lies?"

"Well, if it's so unimportant why does your father have to write an article denouncing Fidel in—"

"He didn't denounce Fidel!"

"He said Fidel was a stooge for the Soviet Union."

"What are you talking about? He didn't say that."

"That's what he said. Read it."

"I have read it. Come on!"

"Well, he says that Fidel is only doing this because he needs the Soviet Union right now because of the crop failures."

Richard stared at her, surprised that her argument made sense and stunned that she had the nerve to say it. Lisa seemed ecstatic to have reduced him to silence. She smiled broadly and delightedly at him, almost as if he should share in her pleasure at his defeat. "Right?" she said, and looked at the others.

"You're out of your fucking mind!" Richard said quickly. He had seen Joan's look of discomfort and he sensed that an attempt would be made to end the discussion. It was obviously unpleasant for the other three. "I can't believe that the one thing in the article which is written to defuse the criticism of Fidel is what you consider so bad."

"What?" Lisa said loudly. "I don't know what you're talking about."

"Lisa, what is this shit?" Salvatore said.

"Yeah," Mark said. "I think it would be better if you two—"

"Oh no!" Richard yelled. "I want her to deal with what I said."

"Fine," Lisa looked at Richard calmly. "I didn't hear what you said."

"Dad explained the relationship between Fidel and the Soviet Union in order to show Fidel's side of it. Clearly Fidel thinks it's more important that the Cuban people eat than that their artists be free to write avant-garde junk."

"Isn't that saying that Fidel is a stooge?"

"*You* are concluding that Fidel is a stooge because he depends on the Soviet Union for food. *You* make that judgment, not Dad."

"Not Dad," she mimicked.

He felt his heart pound and the room's light close in. Lisa even paused momentarily at the ferocity of his expression.

"Well, *Dad,*" she went on with a humorous emphasis, "isn't

making much sense. Because that proves Fidel was right. It's not important what happens to Padilla if it means Cubans will starve."

"And I suppose it doesn't matter that the Soviet—"

"Stop shouting, Richard," Lisa said with an air of innocence that doubled Richard's fury.

"Don't you dare tell me to stop shouting! I'll scream—" He knew he had lost the others from the embarrassment on their faces, and Joan's interruption was a galling confirmation: "Richard. Calm down, it's not worth it."

"Shut up!" he yelled, opening his throat and ripping the sounds out. "Shut up!"

"I can't take this," Joan said, and left.

Mark called after her and followed her out, and Richard watched Salvatore do the same with surprise. He had never had walkouts by observers during a tantrum. Lisa still sat on the floor with her legs crossed and her feet tucked beneath her body, smiling somewhat pityingly at him. "This is silly," she said.

"Will you listen! You're into scoring points. Listen!"

"Okay."

"It means nothing to you that the Soviet Union applies this pressure. You don't care about that. Anything to justify Fidel. Does the Cuban Revolution amount to anything if it's merely an excuse for Soviet power? If they're going to influence tiny decisions such as the status of poets, then what else will they influence? They didn't support Che. I mean, do I have to run down the number of fucked up things Russia has done in terms of leftist movements in other countries. Like the CP in France?"

"You're so confused. I don't know what you're saying." She scored with every line, touching on things about him or his ideas that he felt were embarrassing or irrational. He tried over and over to force her into discussing his points, but she remained personal, saying he was defensive, that he was too upset to think clearly.

He heard the other three laughing in one of the adjoining rooms, and occasionally a head would pop in to see if they were still fighting. He imagined he heard them comment on his stubbornness, and every laugh sounded derisive.

As Richard became more desperate, he began to return Lisa's personal remarks. He called her manipulative when she accused him of defensiveness. His escalation must have caused her really explosive charge. "You're just an intellectual," she said at last. "You don't like the idea of a poet being censored. It's just a liberal hangup."

"I'm an intellectual!" Richard didn't have an angry reaction at first because it was incredible: he had railed against intellectuals in every other argument; he blamed intellectuals for the decadence of contemporary literature; he left school to avoid becoming one. He would have considered it more likely that he was a fascist. "How the hell am I an intellectual?"

For the first time during their fight he was comfortable. There was no unstoppable surge of rage to embarrass him. He smiled sarcastically at her and noticed with a thrill that she suddenly seemed at a loss. "Well, you read books—"

"I read books!" He laughed with real delight. "Boy, you have low standards. You don't read books, I suppose."

"I mean—"

"Only illiterates aren't intellectuals."

"Richard, will you stop being obnoxious? I mean, you relate to the world through books. You're a novelist."

She had stumbled into this line of attack but Richard could see, in her eyes, her determination to maintain it. He asked her if she meant that novelists were intellectuals and noticed, with dismay, that there wasn't the slightest insincerity in her manner when she said yes.

He was hurt. The discussion was no longer merely tactical or excessively vehement. He was hit. "Novelists aren't intellectuals. Don't you know what intellectual means?" He was whining. "An intellectual perceives the world through ideas. A novelist observes and feels experience and then relates it."

He was so obviously upset that even Lisa hesitated before continuing. "Why are you so defensive about it?" she said once more. It was apparently a favorite question, but this time it seemed more apologetic than offensive. "It's not a terrible thing to say, Richard."

He noticed the disturbance before he spoke. He had said how can you say that, twice, before he turned to look at what had gotten Lisa laughing. Joan was entering the room, riding on Salvatore's back. "We come in peace," she kept saying, addressing it to Richard mostly. Mark was behind them, smiling benignly.

"What the fuck do you two assholes think you're doing!" Richard's words broke up the carefree tableau quickly. To abuse them was satisfying. He felt his voice rumble into a storm of words that refreshed his self, his sense of self. "Don't you come fucking around in here while I'm fighting! I don't care how unimportant it seems to you. You think you're cool and intelligent for not being involved. What are you? Too fucking civilized to be able to stand an argument?" Joan had slid off Salvatore and he had looked abashed. Sal muttered that Richard obviously didn't think it was funny. And Joan had said Richard twice in protest. They all looked at him and he thought, Do they think I'm going to stop? "Get the fuck outta here. Right now! I'm tired of patronizing your sensibilities. I'm fighting with Lisa! So fuck off!"

Lisa allowed him to ramble on about how intellectuals weren't artists when they were alone again. She was quite content with what had already been said and she began to say that it was foolish to go on discussing it. He knew he was through. He couldn't judge which was more painful, continuing to talk to Lisa, or facing the others when it was over.

Mark made a joke about the heavyweight championship finally ending when Richard emerged and said to Joan, "I wanna go."

"Do you want me to go with you?" she asked. "I'm an asshole, remember?"

"That's hilarious," Richard said. "Can we go?"

"All right." She looked suddenly vulnerable and walked over to hug him. His mind told him to hold her and that would relieve most of his humiliation and hers, but his body pulled away against orders. She managed a look of pain and annoyance that was remarkable for its complexity.

"Come on," he said, his voice twisted into a whine.

Her eyes stopped pleading. "All right! Calm down."

He knew they would ride home in silence and that he would turn on the television as soon as they arrived. He didn't want to behave peevishly, but he did. He hoped that after an hour or so he would be able to start talking to her and straighten it out, but she fell asleep almost immediately and he was left alone with ceaseless slow-motion replays of the fight.

He lay on his side, slipping into sleep. His mind was busy repeating his argument when he suddenly felt his body slide into space. He fell rapidly and wanted to wake up and move, but couldn't. Fear rushed in on top of the struggle to move and pushed him up with a start.

"Sweetheart, are you all right?" Joan asked. Her eyes were red and one side of her face was streaked from the pillow.

"No. I woke up with a start." He laughed. "I never knew what that meant. That's heavy. It's really unpleasant."

"Poor baby," she said, and wearily moved next to him. He accepted her gratefully and enjoyed the protectiveness of having her head on his chest.

"I wonder why that happened," he said.

"It's probably because we didn't talk about the argument."

"Oh, yeah?" He smiled as he realized that the bitterness he had felt about Joan's behavior had been so quickly repressed. Such knowledge was still too new to be depressing. "Yeah, I was really pissed off at you," he said casually.

"You were very mean, babes," she said, only slightly less casually.

His attempt to absorb and accept this view of hers was intercepted by anger. "Well, that was just defense, you know? I mean, you fucked me up first."

"What?" She moved away and looked at him. "How—" She stopped and then lay down. "It's silly. You were upset."

"Exactly," he said in a loud quick tone.

There was silence and they both huddled into the blankets as if they were going to sleep. Richard's nervousness increased as he remembered Joan entering the room on Sal's back. He couldn't believe she was so ready to ridicule him. "I'm gonna turn out the light, okay?" Joan asked.

"Uh, no. We've got to talk." He said that grimly and tossed the covers aside violently. He got out of bed and hunted in his clothes for cigarettes.

She sat up, looking tired, and watched him. After he lit a cigarette, he stood at the foot of the bed. "I guess you don't understand."

"I don't."

"Yeah. Well, if that had been just a routine political discussion I wouldn't have been right to be so upset that you wanted me to stop. She was talking about my father." He paused and looked intently at her.

Joan returned his look and waited. "Do you want me to say something to that?" she asked at last.

"You don't get it, huh?"

"Richard, I knew she was talking about your father."

"Oh, come on! Fuck off!"

"What? What are you upset about?"

"I suppose you would have been casual about it if it had been your father. I suppose that it means nothing. I suppose it doesn't even mean anything that she called me an intellectual." Joan laughed. "What are you laughing at?" She looked stunned. "She was telling me I came from a family of intellectuals whose liberal perceptions—" He was overwhelmed by frustration. "She was calling me a pig."

"Richard, you're being crazy."

"I'm telling you that's what it amounts to."

"Okay."

She sat quietly, stubbornly. "Look," he said. "Even if you thought I was too upset, then why didn't you respect my problem? Why didn't you just wait it out?"

"I can't answer that. That's not the way I saw it."

"Well, goddammit, how did you see it?"

"Babes, do you have to yell at me?"

"I'm sorry."

"I thought you were very upset and I didn't think you were

doing yourself any good arguing with her. I mean, I thought it was silly to fight about it. We just thought it would break up the tension if we came in like that."

"Yeah, it sure broke the tension. I can't believe you didn't realize that I would think you were ridiculing me."

"You thought I was making fun of you?"

Her expression was so incredulous that he suddenly felt foolish. "Of course. What else do you expect me to think?"

She smiled. "I didn't expect that. You really thought that?"

"Yeah," he said unhappily.

She looked at him lovingly, but with a mild amusement that he fancied contained a trace of contempt. "I'm sorry you thought that, babes, but I didn't—I wasn't making fun of you. I just wanted to stop the argument. So did Sal. He thought Lisa was crazy."

The conversation had taken on a settled tone; Richard walked away from the bed and then back again. "Yeah, but you see she really wasn't being crazy. She was just being straight about her arrogance toward people she considers nonpolitical, or nonactivist."

He watched her reaction to this and it was obvious that Joan merely distrusted the sound of his words and had no understanding of them. "I mean," he went on, "that's the way most of those people feel about me."

"What people?"

"*Political* people." He had snapped the word at her.

"Look. I'm not gonna get into this. I don't know what's freaking you out about this but I can't deal with it. If you want me to support you no matter what happens or what you're saying—I can't do that."

"Oh, then fuck off. Go to sleep." He got into his clothes and she watched him, looking miserable.

"Are you leaving?" she asked plaintively.

He looked at her and laughed. "Boy, do you have an exaggerated sense of the force of my anger! No, you fool, I'm going to read. I just don't want to be cold."

He stayed up until dawn. He considered that an appropriate reaction and woke up to an empty apartment refreshed. Joan had left him a note explaining that she was out job hunting, and he was amused by this unusual care she took to explain her absence. He was pleased they had fought. He was especially pleased he had left her on the defensive. She had always been in control of their relationship because of her greater sexual experience, and he had discovered a major weapon to neutralize her.

CHAPTER NINE

Richard spent the last month of the summer smoking grass and bickering with Joan. They fucked once and he was perfunctory about it. It didn't occur to him that Joan might become disgusted with his behavior. He also refused to analyze why he was so depressed.

In September, they spent one weekend cleaning the apartment. It was unbearable to do such work, but, after Richard had vacuumed and straightened vehemently, he felt his thoughts were just as ordered and clear as the apartment.

They settled on the bed and Joan furtively rubbed his groin and, when encouraged, she undid his pants and lowered them. Richard was heartened by his situation: his penis enveloped in the cool of her mouth, his novel coming out in two months. It was fantastic to consider, to add up, the things he had acquired in the last six months: an apartment, a checking account, a lover, a publisher, a summer vacation, a life ordered by no institution. He knew it was cynical to think of it this way but he did, gleefully and triumphantly. How frightening that that was all he enjoyed about them. The fact of their existence.

He loved it when Joan took his penis into her mouth, but there was something ruthless about looking down at her doing it. He felt it was impolite to enjoy it too much. And then the problem it created by bringing him to a climax. So when it became impossible to control his excitement, he stopped her. She lay back ready for him, and it was difficult to overcome the sudden depression that hit him. It was tawdry: the lights on, his pants bunched at his knees, and Joan lying there with her eyes closed, waiting.

"Babes," he said with a slight tremble.

She opened her eyes, alarmed. "What?"

He got up and put his pants back on. "I don't want to have sex."

He expected an explosion but it was silent, internal. He saw its flash in her eyes. "Why?"

"God, this is so fucking tense." Richard smiled, hoping to get rid of her severe expression. But she only looked more unhappy. "I'm sorry, babes," he said. "I just feel fucked up."

She began to cry! He was amazed. Great tears formed in each eye and rolled down her cheeks. He ran over and hugged her. It did something extraordinary to his privacy, his self-indulgence, when confronted with emotion. Even that brief amusement he felt at being in the middle of a classic scene between men and women was broken through. She sobbed in his arms, he felt his eyes ache and tears come. "I don't know what's happening," Joan said. "I just feel so frustrated." They both laughed at the word. "What's the matter? You can't stand my body?" She was so ashamed to ask that he was saying no before she finished the sentence. And he said no several times while she wept. He realized he had to explain his coldness, the anger he had allowed to silence him for the past weeks.

"I've been shitty because of that argument with Lisa. Wait," he said, to stop her from protesting innocence. "I've always felt inferior in my family about politics. And I don't like feeling inferior." They laughed at this. "Even when Dad was telling us about Padilla, he didn't address himself to *me*, he talked to those schmucks."

"What schmucks?"

"Leo and Louise. What schmucks! Have you got a block about this?"

"Probably."

"Anyway, I'm tired of it, I'm tired of being patronized. I'm tired of being thought of as a little middle-class kid who has no right to be impressive about politics. Mark telling me in Vermont that he's a revolutionary! My brother has been parading around like Lenin for the past three years and they are all little snot-nosed kids."

"That's silly, babes."

"*That's* what got me angry! Don't tell me it's silly. You hurt me badly when you say that. I know it may seem crazy. It isn't important whether I'm right. I feel attacked about being a writer. Not even that. I feel like I'm being treated as some kind of a freak. At least the publication of my novel will stop that. But unless I jump on people for dismissing me on any political question, I'll be miserable."

"Richard, you think about these things in a destructive way. Nobody ignores you. If anything, people are a little frightened of you."

"*You're* frightened of me," he said, laughing. "The others aren't."

"Why should anybody be frightened of you? I mean, why do you want that?"

"Honey, you're making me sound like a gangster. I want *respect,* not fear." He tried to smile at her winningly, but his expression was more like a plea. She looked shyly at him and then impulsively hugged him.

"I respect you," she whispered. "Even though you've given yourself to me."

He laughed wildly at her joke and was excited by even this pretense that she could compulsively get him to bed. He immediately began to take her clothes off but she took over that task so that they could quickly be naked. He was delighted by the recklessness of their acts and it inspired him to dive toward her cunt. He had always hesitated to put his mouth there; there, at the center of the world—hairy, odorous, full of an unconquerable desire. He thought of it this way while crouched before it: in overwhelming, alienating metaphors.

She lay back and enjoyed his kisses and tonguing as if he

were a dutiful pet. What he imagined her feelings to be while she touched his genitals were really his: he resented her pleasure, her passive acceptance of his self-abnegation. He worked carefully, methodically, at bringing her to a climax. And finally entered her for his own, by now jaded, ecstasy. But she was much happier after they had intercourse this way, even though it was clear to her that he didn't enjoy it. Richard concluded that fucking was one-sided in this peculiar sense and understood why so many people seemed to be flailing about intellectually on the subject. He felt it was to his credit that he had faced the truth so quickly.

Early fall was Richard's happiest time. He and Joan had their honeymoon, financed by his novel's advance: their life was lazy and occupied by fucking.

But, in late October, his career reached a climax that lasted for a month. His novel appeared in the stores and was reviewed in papers around the country, including those he had read daily in what he came to think of as that other miserable obscure existence.

At last—all anyone talked about was his life and his novel. His parents called every other day to hear the latest review or tell him of someone else's praise. At first it seemed as if there would be no limit to his success, but finally boundaries appeared—after a month his book began to be missed from the shelves and there were no more reviews in the morning mail or friends to tell him how good his novel was.

It was an exhilarating high, like nothing else he had experienced, and its collapse was terrible. He took it, physically, as badly as if it were a hangover. He woke up in the late afternoons with a grogginess it took hours to fight off. He felt stupefied until late at night when nervousness and regret over the wasted day kept him awake talking compulsively to Joan about his ideas for the "future of literature." He would promise himself that he'd get up early and write, but Joan's efforts to rouse him were shrugged off angrily until she refused to try any more.

Everyone else was pleased by his novel's results and thought his life well taken care of. He could go to college if he wished or just get an advance on his second book and write.

Richard couldn't accept that a year's work and a year's wait —a whole life of anticipation—were over in four weeks.

The change in people's attitudes toward him was at first a delight, a delicate revenge. When he saw Mark at his brother's apartment during the week his book was published he nearly burst out laughing at the humble manner that Mark adopted while telling him how "Joycean and painful your novel is. You deal really correctly with middle-class alienation."

Richard had to look long at Mark's face, and even then he couldn't believe it. "Do you mean that or are you just kidding me?"

Lisa interrupted Mark's answer. "Kidding! He's been talking to me about it for two days." She began saying something about how funny his book was but he heard only his own thought, like a voice-over in a movie: "So it takes a capitalist publishing house to stamp my ideas with approval so that you'll respect them."

Later, a man asked Richard what he did in a bored tone, and when Richard said he was a novelist the man seemed even more indifferent. Richard pictured how he appeared to this stranger: his hair long and unwashed, his shirt wrinkled, his jeans almost thoughtfully splashed with paint stains, and above all, the boyish face. "Have you published anything?" the man asked.

Richard had thought he wanted a final proof of contempt, because he could shatter it so effortlessly, but this acting out of what he knew intellectually, that he was nothing unpublished and everything once in print, was depressing. "Yes, my first novel was just published." Richard had flashed his credentials but the man, after a start, wanted a closer look.

"Who published it?"

This was still asked with a trace of condescension, and Richard needed a moment before realizing that the man expected a university press or something equally small and comforting. Richard snapped his publisher's name like a whip and at last brought the stranger to attention.

This scene was repeated so often that he forgot why it depressed him and would feel only a dulled embarrassment—as if he were merely too sensitive and should bear the blame for the small shocks that information of his career caused. People asked him, shortly after being introduced, how much money he was earning. On one occasion, when he responded by saying it wasn't enough, he received a lecture that he would end up vulgarizing his novels in order to make enough money.

So the family gathering in Vermont was a relaxing prospect. He would not have to explain himself. Richard and Joan went up with his brother and Louise, and he was surprised by Leo's comment as the car pulled away from their apartment house. "Well, here we go, like lambs to the slaughter."

"No, no," said Louise, looking at Richard. "It's going to be nice, won't it?"

"I've really been looking forward to it," he said so solemnly that Leo laughed, thinking Richard had meant it sardonically. After a moment of confusion, Richard said, "I mean it. I expect it to be great."

Leo seemed embarrassed and Louise said, "Yes, I hope so. I think we'll have fun. We'll try to, right?"

Her tone was suspiciously pointed, and Richard glanced at Joan to see if she was having the same reaction. But she just looked tired from rising early. It was a miserable gray morning, the sky unfinished and disgruntled. He felt a chill and leaned back against Joan, falling into a fitful sleep while they swung gracefully through the moody slopes and turns of the Saw Mill River Parkway. Richard thought intermittently about Louise's puzzling comment, and when he finally sat up to waken fully, he asked, "You two aren't looking forward to this, huh?"

This was greeted with a pause that endured too long to be meaningless. Leo glanced at Louise before answering. "You know, man, with all of us together—John and Naomi—it could become one of those psychodramas."

"You know how Aaron gets when he has all the kids together," Louise said, and then addressed Joan: "Aaron is one of

136

the most intelligent and sophisticated men I know, but when he gathers his dear children—"

"He becomes a basket case," Leo said.

"No," Louise said quickly, "he becomes"—she moved her hand in the air several times, searching for the word—"neurotically self-important. You know, that parent thing where he tries to make everything reflect on his being Big Daddy."

Richard watched Joan's neutral reaction to this information and remembered the romantic picture he had given her of his relationship with Aaron. He had turned Aaron's casually arrogant judgments on literature into a massive intellectual domination that would fit nicely with Louise's comments. It would be useless to try to wipe all that out with a one-liner like, "We're the neurotics, because we can't admit we are his children."

After all, he realized later when they had almost reached their destination, I'm sensitive about it because I feel guilty that I unfairly criticized Dad. I wouldn't argue with them for his sake.

But it took the warmth out of the hugging when they arrived. It seemed sinister to Richard, watching Leo and Louise embrace his father, particularly since they did so with more enthusiasm than he could muster.

The routine of arrival—the hellos, the tours of the grounds to see improvements, a series of bathroom visits, and the eating—had this difference: Joan. Richard was excited for the first time while the house and grounds were toured. He wanted her to love them, to think of the property as he did, the home where they would eventually live, the first sanctuary for the long line of peasants who made up his ancestry. But he was not disappointed when she obviously thought of the place as his parents', behaving politely and wearily. He still had the pleasure of someone's hand to hold while they sat around the kitchen table snacking.

They were expecting John and Naomi in a few hours, and when every one of the travelers, except for Richard, decided to take naps, Richard followed Betty while she cleared the kitchen table and wrapped the leftovers.

"Well, Mom, do you like the girl I've brought home?"

Betty smiled naturally at his blunt and foolish question. "I haven't had a chance to talk to her."

"I know," he said. "You hate her. Well, it's only my first try."

"Oh, I see. You're in a silly mood."

He paced about the kitchen trying to figure out what state he was in. "I'm restless," he announced after some thought. It seemed profound.

"What about?"

"Don't ask hard questions. Maybe for John and Naomi to arrive. I haven't seen them for almost a year."

"That's right," Betty said. She had put the dishes, after a pretty thorough cleaning, in the dishwasher and had finished wiping the counters. "Well, now that I've cleaned it all up, I'll make dinner."

Richard laughed. "I can appreciate that now, Mom. If I were you, I'd suggest going out to eat."

"Are you eating out a lot in New York?"

"Yeah, yeah. It's bad. I know. You've seen John and Naomi recently?"

"Oh! Change the subject, did you? Yes, I saw them in the fall. I went there for a week."

"And is their relationship—well, how did it seem?"

She stopped her activity and looked at Richard. "You know, Naomi says you're the only one who understands why they separated."

"They *didn't* separate. Isn't that part of why I understood it."

"What?"

"Naomi told me that everybody in the family insisted on thinking of it as a *separation*. You know, in the sense of *divorce*. To divide, etc."

"All right, don't be such a wise guy."

"I'm not. That's the way she felt. That people presumed their vacation from each other was just the first step toward divorce."

"But nobody said anything like that to her."

"Oh, come on, Mom. Leo said to me once, 'That fucking brother-in-law of ours better not pull a WASP on Naomi and try to leave her without a penny.'"

Betty shook her head in irritation and Richard saw a warning signal he had learned to fear over the years: her eyes clouding with tears and anger. He was taking this subject too lightly. "Oh, that's just Leo's nonsense. *I* never said—"

"Mom! Mom," Richard said quickly, hurrying over to Betty and patting her arm. He knew the gesture showed his terror of her feelings more than it really comforted her, but he never realized that until he found himself stroking her arm hurriedly, wishing he could withdraw what he had just said.

"I never said anything like that to her," Betty said, and then smiled knowingly, perhaps a little bitterly, at him. "It's all right, Richard, I'm in control of myself." She compensated for this cut by kissing him on the forehead and then returning to the dinner's preparation.

They were silent until Richard heard Leo's voice announcing that he was taking a shower. "What did he say?" Betty asked.

"He's taking a shower so don't use the hot water." The subject seemed closed, but Richard, watching approaching gloom of a winter's night at one of the windows, felt chastised for his frivolous attitude. He couldn't understand why he had cared so little about Naomi's crisis, and it only made him feel more shallow that his casualness had been mistaken for understanding by Naomi. The rest of the family had buzzed about, gossiping and steeling themselves for a massed rejection of John, because they assumed Naomi would need all the support —including malice toward John—that love can give a young divorced mother. He conjured up the image that they must have had then: of Naomi, almost collapsing from her child's weight, trudging off manless in the snow.

"It's very hard being a mother with a little baby," Betty said in the middle of tasting a sauce. She replaced the lid of a pot on the stove and bent over to check the flame. "There's a terrible amount of pressure on you. It makes your marriage very difficult."

"I *know*," Richard said, his irritation surprising him and Betty.

"Don't be annoyed," she said, not commanding.

He wanted to yell self-righteously about his needs, but he'd learned the value of cautious statements. "You don't need to sell me on having consideration and sympathy for my sister, Mom. She's done a pretty good job of that." Betty looked at him with her expression changing slowly from apology to disapproval. "Oh, don't look at me like that," he said. "I haven't had a shot at oppressing anybody, do you know that? I was never allowed to be unconsciously racist, sexist, or just plain unconscious." He stopped because it was turning into a tirade.

"Oh, you're just being silly and cantankerous."

There was always this moment in disagreements with members of his family. The rush of fury, like a car engine flooding, the wheels racing uselessly. I *have* to understand this too, he thought. It's her daughter, her self reincarnate. His parents had fought when Naomi was a teen-ager, and Aaron had insisted she wash the dishes. "No daughter of mine is going to wash dishes," Betty yelled. Oh, how boring people really were, Richard thought. This is my mother's mysterious inner life—she doesn't want her daughter to be a victim of male chauvinism. How could he tell his mother how tough it was for him, without whining or belittling the profound nature of his sister's problems? "There's a lot of pressures on me too," he said, and knew immediately that it was inadequate.

"Well, of course, it's very hard being a writer. I told you not to be one." She smiled at him with an embarrassing and comforting love. "But it's nothing like having a child. Another living being who depends on you every hour of every day. You're never free of it."

He stared at her, at it. The feeling, the scene. "I'll see you later," he said, and walked through the pantry, leaving the house.

"You don't have a coat," she called after him.

There had been no snow for weeks so it was cold and empty outdoors, the ground gray and frozen, the trees, except for the evergreens, bare. He stared at this scene for a moment before deciding to run the length of the driveway. It was too cold to walk. His feet were hurt by the hard matted ground and his steps echoed loudly in the forest. He had a feeling that he would meet John and Naomi on the driveway and, indeed, their car turned in it just as he began his slow trot back.

John stopped the car and they did their hugging and kissing out in front of it. Richard pretended interest in his young niece to avoid conversation, but after holding her in his arms he became hopelessly sentimental and kissed her repeatedly on the forehead so that Naomi said, "Oh, you're necking. That's what I do with her all the time."

Richard had no chance to respond because they had reached the house. It was funny to watch the family all come out through the door together, almost fighting to reach them first. He remembered Joan was a stranger and would need his escort, so he handed Nana to Betty and hurried into the house. He found Joan standing in the pantry brushing her hair self-consciously. She smiled with relief when he appeared and he loved her deeply for that.

He led her outside and toward the family group, and only then did he become aware of how nervous he was about his family's judgment of Joan. And from the expression on Naomi's face, she was voraciously interested in what he had come up with. Naomi broke in immediately after Richard introduced them, "So this is my little brother's girl friend."

"Yeah," Richard said. "We fuck like grownups, you know."

His remark caused a commotion but it was nothing like the shock he had expected, and despite the embarrassment that instantly overwhelmed him, he wished it had upset them more. Joan saved him from both feelings, however, when she said, "It might be better if we were more childish about it."

"Oh, dear," Aaron said. "I don't think I should be hearing this conversation."

"But you're just the person who I've wanted to talk to about this," Joan said amidst the now relaxed laughter.

"Well," Aaron said. "Don't blame me for any sexual problems. It's his mother's fault, I'm sure."

"The same old story," Betty said.

Joan got along so well with his parents and Naomi and John that he was a little disappointed. She fit in perfectly with their casual teasing, and he watched in disbelief as his mother actually brought out his baby pictures. He was genuinely charmed by this foolish exhibition of love: all of them laughing and smiling at photographs of him, looking up every few minutes to check on the final product. But he felt, with an acuteness and distance he hadn't achieved ever before, the irritation of being young, of being cute, of having easy problems, of having a quick access to talent.

When they had all retired for the night, Richard noticed the light on in his father's study and he excused himself from Joan and went there. Aaron looked up at him as he entered, and the look on his face made Richard feel, for a moment, that there was nothing bothering him.

"Can we talk? Am I interrupting?"

"Sure, fellow," Aaron said with one of those reflective smiles that both pleased and suffocated.

"I seem like a pretty big success, don't I?" Richard asked.

"Ah, not so big."

He was immediately annoyed. "Are you serious!"

"Of course, you're a big success. You need to be told that?" Aaron seemed to think of something. "Haven't I told you how good that novel is?"

"Oh yeah," Richard said, and then laughed at himself. "I was ready to blow up at you for not thinking I was a success."

"But I—"

"I know, I know. What's funny, or what's sad, I should say, is that I came in to complain about my success, or lack of it."

"You mean, your book wasn't successful enough?"

"Yeah," Richard said hesitantly. "Well, it's not that simple. It didn't mean what I thought it would."

"Oh," Aaron said, and looked at him encouragingly. "It never does, you know. What one wants is never the answer to all one's problems."

"I know, I know. I've always read that. I think it was *Anna Karenina* that first taught me that. I longed and longed for her to run off with Vronsky. I guess, subliminally, I thought it would be like a Dickens novel. After the conflict, happiness. I still resent and disbelieve her suicide."

"Well," Aaron said, lowering his voice so it wouldn't seem like a lecture. "It's because she's transgressed society's rules." Aaron wanted to elaborate and he would have in the past. Richard had strained to achieve so that he wouldn't need to be taught such things, and now he regretted having squashed his father's impulse to guide him. "You haven't," Aaron said.

"Oh, I have."

"You're another Karenina?" Aaron said with a laugh. "I don't think so. You've just flaunted the rules a little. And she, after all, cut off her future while you have guaranteed yours." Aaron watched Richard's reaction to this. "Right? Or maybe not. I don't know, maybe you don't want to be a writer."

"Do I have a choice now? I mean a choice that allows me the sickening ego gratification I need. Of course I can grow organic vegetables."

Aaron leaned forward and slapped his knee. "Listen. There are countless things, important things, you can do, and do brilliantly. Without even giving up writing. I'm talking about—"

"I know. Please don't list them. They embarrass me."

"They do?" Aaron was amazed. "Well, tell me what bothers you. I'm talking too much, I'm not letting you speak."

"Okay." Richard let himself think for a moment. He wanted to be clear and totally honest. "I want, I've always wanted, to be the most important writer alive. *Novelist*, not writer. Nothing else means that much, though of course I may like doing them more. I hold you responsible for that. I don't *blame* you for it, but the way you brought me up, the way you talked about novelists made any other profession a cop out. I don't mean this has been forced on me. It was given to me and I began to force it, to push it. I made myself develop contempt for any nonartistic profession, and then I slowly began to loathe the other arts as well. It's a genuine revulsion. I can't complete myself or my life without writing novels."

"But you're doing that."

"If I hadn't been published for another ten years then perhaps what's just happened would have pleased me for quite a while. Dad, I never wrote anything longer than three pages until my first novel. You know that. It was published immediately. The *instantness* of it. God, I expected to be embalmed the way Bellow is, or whoever. I'm emotionally ready for the end. The retirement to the country, the National Book Award, the fifteen published novels, the honorary degrees, a Writer's in Residence, the starry-eyed coeds wanting to fuck me, the Ph.D.s being done on my work, long careful discussions of my influence in *The New York Review of Books*."

"*That* too," Aaron said, laughing. "You're asking for a lot."

"After one crumby novel. You're damn right. I think I was overpraised."

"Oh no you weren't. Don't believe that!"

"Well, that's what I'm afraid they'll think. That they made it too easy for me. That they'll make the rest of my life miserable by saying I haven't lived up to my potential. Or worse, that out of desperation I'll start writing those fake modern novels with glittering prose surfaces, so mystifying that they won't dare to say they're empty novels."

"That's not going to happen. You have too much self-awareness for that. In fact, you have too much self-awareness. Relax. Your work is good, and you're very young, and frankly, after forty years of work, I think you'll probably have all those things."

"But don't you see that if I don't get those things, I'll be horribly crushed? And if this hadn't happened to me, being a *prodigy*"—he stopped and looked disgusted—"I should never have thought that my chances were so good to be what I want. I could have dismissed it as a wild fantasy. But from now on, I'll always feel that I had my chance and blew it."

Betty appeared at the door wearing a long robe. "Are you two fighting?"

"No, no," Aaron said. "Come in. I'm afraid our son is feeling the burdens of the world too much."

"Ah," Betty sighed, and went over to Richard, brushing his hair back from his brow and bending to kiss him on the forehead. "My poor son."

He felt queasy and ready to cry. He wanted to say how

scared, how incompetent he felt to live up to this life, this deadening progression of success. But the moment for releasing those feelings was past and now he could only force them self-consciously.

"Richard," Aaron said, "if you think about your situation the way you just described it, I think you're right, I think it will become harder and harder for you to work. You're like me, you become the person you're talking to, and so you've read all those reviews about being a boy genius and you've taken on the tragic part. That's what people love to think about extraordinary young artists. That they're doomed or that they're freaks who will always be unhappy. Hasn't everyone been hinting at that?"

"Yeah," Richard said.

"Well, the fact of the matter is that most of the great writers began publishing their novels in their twenties and had begun writing as teen-agers. In fact, if you had not written a novel by now I should doubt seriously that you'd ever be a writer."

Richard began to laugh tearfully at this absurdity along with Betty, who said, "And I was listening so seriously to you!"

"But I was serious," Aaron said. "In my fashion. Having achieved young doesn't doom one to neurosis and failure. Most successful people are successful when young. That's all. Richard, I mean that. In an odd way you have lived a more sane and healthy life than anyone. You did what you wanted to do. And unlike Anna Karenina, there's something a little more meaningful about what you did than simply screwing the person you want to. It doesn't matter if you get those honors you want. You have done everything to get them and that alone is a satisfying thing. You're just feeling the blues from having gone through such a momentous existence for a few months, and now everything is back to normal and it seems duller than ever. That will pass."

"So the work is innocent, right?"

"What?"

"I never told you I found that in my contract?" Richard

asked. "Quote, The Author warrants that The work is innocent, and contains no matter whatsoever that is obscene, libelous, in violation of any right of privacy, or otherwise in contravention of law, unquote."

CHAPTER TEN

It was the fanciest Christmas Richard's family had staged in years. The shopping trips seemed endless as more and more dishes and drinks were found in cookbooks or remembered from novels and movies. Buying presents, though hectic, couldn't compare to the confusion in the kitchen. The stove didn't rest, even when they did, so, for once, Richard's late night schedule not only met with approval from his parents, but with great thanks, as he was charged with checking on various pastries—turning the stove on and off at unlikely times. The night before Christmas Eve his mother asked him to stay up until 2:00 A.M. to keep something from burning. John, after everyone else was in bed, joined him in the kitchen and Richard suggested slyly that they drink some of the rum for the eggnog.

"No," John said. "We might get carried away. Let's stick to the liqueurs."

"Yeah, but they use them in the cakes. I think."

"They only use a little." John went into the living room and returned with a bottle and two brandy glasses.

"Don't pour me too much," Richard said. "I can't afford to try and outdrink you. Besides, getting drunk is the worst sensation in the world."

"Especially the way you go about it."

"Well," Richard said, annoyed. "I was a kid. I wanted to prove something. I *hope* it wasn't my masculinity. That's a hopeless cause." He sipped his drink. "Wow. What's this?"

"Cointreau. To Live. To Love. To Laugh. Cointreau."

Richard laughed. "Oh, that's right. Those ads." He watched John light a cigarette before saying, "It's been a long time since we did this."

John nodded slowly, deliberately. "Too long."

"Well, you know what happened to me. So?"

John scratched his beard. "Your life is a matter of public record." Richard chuckled politely and John, after a moment's thought, continued, "Things have been good. Better than ever."

"I heard that. How come?"

John smiled knowingly. "You're pretty nosy."

"Oh, come on. What am I supposed to do? Pretend our conversations never happened? You were not happy. Now you are. Why?"

"Boy, this family! Everything's got to come out." Richard began to object, but John hurried on. "You were the best about it, actually. I mean, your folks went nuts about Naomi going to Europe."

"They were worried."

"More than that." He looked at Richard. "You know? They thought I was gonna desert her, or something."

"They just thought you were divorcing. Obviously they're gonna support their daughter, right?"

"But we weren't."

"I know," Richard said, not only to inform but also to prevent John from explaining that distinction. "I'm just trying to get across the idea that my parents still love you, and did then, it's just that they thought Naomi was in big trouble and needed unilateral support."

"Well, they went overboard. They also didn't trust us, didn't trust what we were telling them."

"That's true," Richard said, and then felt amused scorn for himself, since he had sworn just recently that he would refuse to see both points of view. "Fuck it. Who cares? That's your problem and theirs. I have my own difficulties with them." John looked astonished and Richard tried to soften it. "I just want to know, in a friendly way, what's changed that's made things so pleasant."

"We worked out a lot of the tension about the house and taking care of Nana."

"You mean, you made arrangements like who takes care of her when—"

"Right. So that Naomi has time to be alone and, anyway, she's going to get a job counseling people. As part of the poverty program."

"Really? How come nobody told me that?"

"You haven't been in touch with us."

"Yeah, I know. I'm sorry, but things have been really, uh, absorbing." John asked Richard to tell him about the novel's publication, and Richard got through it rather quickly. His story, including explanations of the influence of various events, had been made succinct by frequent practice.

They continued drinking, John at a rate that Richard didn't bother to pretend he could equal. Richard's sipping was steady, nevertheless, and he felt the delicious wooziness and indifference that characterized the only safe kind of drunkenness he could achieve. They talked about the other times they drank with an air of sad nostalgic longing, and an ignorant observer would have thought Richard wanted a return to those nights with John when he talked compulsively—elaborately and romantically—about his feelings. What he really wanted, and the reason for his encouraging John to think he had enjoyed those bouts, was John's good opinion, and Richard knew the key to that was deceiving John about the good old days.

The following morning, Christmas Eve, Richard woke up late with a hangover and enjoyed the care he received first from Joan and then from his mother, whose opening line upon seeing him was, "So looking after my cooking drove you to drink."

She was serving him lentil soup in the kitchen and his father looked in from the living room, the *Times* in one hand and his glasses perched on the end of his nose. "You know," he said to

Richard. "In our discussion the other night I forgot to mention that you mustn't become an alcoholic."

"Shucks, Dad, you told me too late." Richard enjoyed this casual attention to his degeneracy. "How did you know we were drinking?" he asked Betty.

"John made a joke about it when he got up with the baby in the morning."

So he was open about it, Richard thought. "He got up with the baby? The man's body is amazing."

"Why?" Betty asked with a look of concern. "Did you two drink a lot?"

"Ah ha!" Richard laughed and looked at Joan. "You see, she was faking this lack of interest. Just trying to wheedle it out of me."

"I knew she was trying that all along," Joan said.

"Don't worry, Mom. We didn't drink that much. Two glasses of wine give me a hangover."

"John had stopped drinking before he came here, so don't you get him started again."

"*Me* get him started. Oh boy, I'm in trouble. Listen, Mom, what is it? What did I do? Is my room not clean enough?"

"Am I being too hard on you?"

Richard nodded bashfully and got a loud smacking kiss from Betty on the forehead. Joan looked at him and was ready with a sarcastic remark when Naomi entered, walking briskly, dressed in boots and a heavy overcoat. "Brother," she said. "Come, let's take a walk."

Betty protested that he hadn't finished eating, but Richard, after another curt request from Naomi, hurried both his breakfast and his dressing for the cold outdoors. They went out and Naomi took his arm. "Shall we walk to the road?" she asked.

"Sure. Is there something in particular we're going to discuss?"

"No," she said, suddenly relaxed. "I just haven't seen my snuggums brother for a long time."

"My God," Richard said, embarrassed. "You're not gonna start using my childhood names."

"Oh, I'm sorry." Naomi was abject. "I forgot. That must be very annoying. I'm sorry."

He laughed. "It didn't upset me. In fact, I rather like the idea of going back to my baby names. It's comforting."

"I'm glad," she said, turning girlishly to look at him before resuming their walk. "It's sad that you're all grown up."

"Is it really?"

"Yeah," Naomi said quietly.

Richard respected the silence Naomi wanted after that statement. He knew from past experience with her that this sadness was not serious. He watched the gray sky through the branches of the sleeping trees, hoping for snow.

"So are you going to become very famous?" she asked finally.

He tried to look clever, self-knowing. But Naomi's expression was earnest. "Do you mean, is that what I'm trying to do?"

Her eyes watched him thoughtfully. "I guess so."

"Yeah. Of course that's what I'm trying to do."

"Really?" she asked in a tone of surprise that seemed ready to become shock.

"Well, Naomi," he said, irritated, "you've put it unfairly. I want to write beautiful, brilliant novels that encompass all of human experience. I don't want to be famous for writing junk. I want to be famous for being great."

"Oh, all right."

He laughed. "That's all right? Good."

"No. I just thought maybe being published and everything had distorted your, you know, sense of what you want."

Of course it had, he thought, but why is that her business? Triumph and defeat are private matters of the spirit. "No, I'm still a serious artist. I still have my ecstasies, you know?" He smiled and hoped to cheer her out of this romantic melancholy.

She laughed and tugged at his arm excitedly. "That's good. That's what I wanted to know."

"So what's with you? I hear you're gonna get a job."

"Well, I might, I'm not sure."

They had reached the end of the driveway and they stopped as if waiting for someone to arrive. Richard, looking up and down the empty roadway, got the feeling that no car would come for months. "You mean, you don't know if you'll get it?" he asked.

"Oh, I'll get it," she said with surprise. "I've got it. I mean, they offered it to me. I don't know—" She broke off and stared ahead with no indication of ever resuming.

"You have a reason for not wanting to work?"

Naomi was delighted. "Sure. Who wants to work? No, I do, but—I don't know if I should."

"The baby. Is that it?"

"Yeah," she said abstractedly, and Richard didn't encourage any further discussion. He was tired of feeling sympathetic to the needs of women.

"I'm told things are good between you and John," he said.

"Is that what people do in this family!" Naomi said with stunning irritation. "Check on how my marriage is going?"

"Hey! I'm just—it's part of your life. You don't want me to ask about it?"

"No," she said in a whine near to tears. "Who told you that?"

"What?"

"That we were doing well."

"John. Who else for Christ's sake!"

This hit her forcefully and she embraced him, saying, "I'm sorry, I'm crazy." She broke away. "Let's go back to the house. I'm in a terrible mood, I need some nice tea."

They turned to walk back. "I asked him last night," Richard said in a hurried tone. "And he said things had really been good, so I just wanted, I don't know, to enjoy that with you."

"Enjoy that with me?"

"Well, it sounded very nice the way he said it. I thought we could have a pleasant time discussing it." He tried to smile ingratiatingly at her.

"I don't know why I did that," she said. "I just feel the whole family's talking behind my back about us."

He wanted to tell her how natural and good it was that people worried about them, but he'd learned how useless it was to try to make the world objective and sensible. "No," he lied. "No one's said a word."

"Good," she said, shaking off her ill feelings immediately and looking adventurously at him. "So you want to know why things are so good? I taught John to argue."

Richard laughed.

"I shouldn't say that. I encouraged him to get angry. To fight. He wasn't brought up to fight. You know what I mean? I always felt in our family, for whatever else was wrong, we knew how to fight, how to get angry at each other. But his parents only argue when they're drunk and then it's just forgotten or dismissed in the morning."

"Hey, that's good. That sounds like you're really dealing with stuff." Richard listened to this new self of his talk with revulsion—but a revulsion that could diminish.

"Oh yeah," Naomi said tenderly. "It was good for us to live apart. That's what nobody, except for you, understood."

Richard spent the long afternoon, made longer by frantic preparations for a huge meal and the wrapping of presents, having intimate talks. Leo collared him to help gather wood for the fireplace.

But, once in the barn, Leo asked him why Aaron was so upset with him. Richard asked what he meant and Leo complained that Aaron teased him about his lack of a career. "Well, you started that bullshit about being a bum," Richard said. Leo looked afraid and Richard softened his tone. "Remember when you were busy with the Columbia uprising and you thought it was clever to answer the question of what you were doing by saying, Oh, I'm just a bum?"

"It was a great tactic," Leo said happily. "Because it would put people back on the defensive. They'd have to start encouraging me and making me feel better about doing political work."

"Yeah, it was cute. But Mom and Dad took it very seriously and thought you shouldn't belittle yourself. Now Dad's figured out that you were being perverse and so now he's on your ass. It's his tactic."

Richard had disappointed Leo as an analyst. "No, man. It has to do with your book." Richard told himself to go on alert and repel any pain. Leo whispered, "He's afraid that I feel bad. That's why he keeps encouraging me to do that jail stuff into a book."

Richard wanted to remind Leo that he had mentioned it first to Aaron. But instead he listened patiently and said, "I guess so," to each elaborate scenario Leo created to explain Aaron's attitude. Richard found it difficult, but it pleased Leo to have him agree.

When they returned to the living room Richard was upset even more by Louise. She had never forgotten the fights Richard used to have with Aaron and, for the last few days, had spent a lot of time whispering asides to Richard when Aaron would slap him on the back and tell him to stand up straight, or suggest he brush his teeth. Richard hated her for it: he was enraged by her assumption that he was oppressed by the duties of a son. She imitated Aaron as they came in carrying the wood, calling Richard "dear boy" with the tone of an English patrician. "Dear boy, would you feed the dog. Oh, I'm so grateful. Your old man is so grateful having such a dutiful son." He stared at her coldly but she continued, seemingly unruffled. She obviously remembered when Richard used to imitate Aaron and thought it relieved him to make fun of his father.

He escaped by joining his mother in her room where she was writing out cards for the presents. He told her about Louise's behavior, frustrated at his inability to stop her without a fight.

"That's the way people are, Richard," she said. "They never get it out of their heads if you tell them something about yourself."

"My God, I wrote a whole novel full of feelings that I no longer have and everybody assumes I've still got them. There are people who seriously ask me if I ever see my parents. It's bad enough they assume everything in it is true of me, but at least they could realize I'm bound to change in five years."

"Well," she smiled. "They won't."

"Sorry, huh? I just gotta take it."

"It has its advantages, doesn't it? Don't let that bother you. So Louise has made up some crazy story in her brain about you and your father. She's a good friend of yours. She means you no harm."

"She thinks Leo is under constant attack in this family. You know that, don't you?"

"Well, she loves him."

"It drives me crazy. She protects us all. That hopeless neurotic protecting us! There, you see. She makes me talk like her. How do I know she's neurotic?"

"Who isn't?" Betty laughed, delighted with the thought. "Don't let it bother you. It doesn't affect your father, you realize that?"

"No. That's why it bothers me. I'm unhappy that Dad and I had so much trouble about school."

"You were right about school. He doesn't bear you any ill will for that. He's very proud of you."

Richard was pleased to hear her say so, but embarrassed by the intensity of the satisfaction. "Anyway, it bothers me. I've been able to straighten things out with Dad and she won't, the *world* won't, realize it."

"That's what you get for being such a wise guy and publishing a novel."

Betty got him to laugh and relax about it so that when he rejoined the group downstairs he could tell himself that he'd let Louise retain her fantasy world in which Richard was harassed by his father, overprotected by his mother, all of them burdened with guilt and repressed anger. He wasn't upset by the faces she made at Aaron's admiration of John's work while they had their huge meal. He knew she was thinking of what she had once told him: that his parents had hit Leo over the head with John's hard work while they thought of Leo as a bum. He would have fought her so hard in the past. But he would have been forgiven for vehemence as an adolescent. He had the innate power of an adult now and must practice nuclear restraint.

He watched as they sat about the table, feeling the strength and independence that Joan's presence gave him, and listened to the secret thoughts that he knew ran like the currents of a stream beneath the quiet surface of their conversation—like a brook babbling now, but it used to have the deafening roar of the ocean's surf.

He felt absolutely different. He watched all night while they played charades, the house busy with their laughter and inventiveness. He studied them one by one while they performed. Their faults and virtues popped up in his mind's eye like sums on a cash register.

He thought his own pantomime was apt, his silence about their faults, and his own, the saving device that life gives. He sat with Joan while she laughed at their antics, at the masks they put on, and decided to believe in those mock faces along with her.

This was life's sadness—standing mute before the people one loves. He had lost his awe of them but he was freed of its bewilderment. Naomi was not Tolstoy, a forbidding hypocritical philosopher who had to be either overthrown or obeyed without question. Beckett's beautiful understanding of silence, her paranoid hatred of New York, her naïveté about the corruption and decadence of American life didn't have to be believed or fought. It was absurd that he had been unable to see her plainly without feeling guilt over his discoveries. It was possible to love her only by accepting those things without contempt, without terror at losing a prophet.

He had lived in a wax museum of heroes. Leo playing Fidel to his Raul, Naomi's Don Juan to his Castaneda, John's cool masculine instincts to his Jewish schleppiness. He had blamed them for their melting under the steady, dull heat of reality. He couldn't face what was weak and ridiculous in people.

But he had had to face it in himself.

R3